But she did. And when she turned to face him, she almost fell from the stool on which she'd been standing. For a moment she teetered precariously, arms flailing, as she tried to regain her balance.

Within an instant, Chance stepped forward and gathered Kylie in his arms. "Are you okay?"

The soft, husky words from Chance's lips fanned against her temple and changed the heat of her embarrassment to something else entirely.

"Yes, I'm fine," she said. "It's just that you...startled me."

He simply nodded, but continued to hold her.

"I'm okay, Chance. You can put me down now," she said, although her voice lacked the conviction to persuade him to do so.

"Are you sure?"

No, Kylie thought. *I'm not sure*. And as much as she wanted to wipe the arrogant smirk from his lips, desire—the likes of which she'd never experienced before—raced through her, igniting her awareness and testing her resolve....

Books by Brenda Jackson

Silhouette Desire

BRENDA JACKSON

is a die "heart" romantic who married her childhood sweetheart and still proudly wears the "going steady" ring he gave her when she was fifteen. Because she's always believed in the power of love, Brenda's stories always have happy endings. In her real-life love story, Brenda and her husband of thirty-three years live in Jacksonville, Florida, and have two sons.

A *USA TODAY* bestselling author, Brenda divides her time between family, writing and working in management at a major insurance company. You may write to Brenda at P.O. Box 28267, Jacksonville, Florida 32226, or by e-mail at WriterBJackson@aol.com or visit her Web site at www.brendajackson.net.

BRENDA JACKSON

solidSOUL

KIMANI PRESS™

ISBN-13: 978-1-58314-770-2
ISBN-10: 1-58314-770-5

SOLID SOUL

www.kimanipress.com

Printed in U.S.A.

Dear Reader,

I love writing family sagas, so it is with great pleasure that I bring you another family to join the Madaris family and the Westmorelands. Meet the Steeles of North Carolina—four brothers and their three female cousins. They are a family of strong, passionate people that are FORGED OF STEELE.

I am very proud that this first book in the series—*Solid Soul*—is my fortieth romance story. Not only am I introducing a new family to my readers while celebrating my fortieth novel, I am also thrilled to be part of the launch of Kimani Romance, Harlequin's new line of African-American love stories.

One of my favorite movies is *The Parent Trap*, and in *Solid Soul* I did a little parent trapping of my own. In this story, two teenagers decide their parents, wealthy businessman Chance Steele and shop owner Kylie Hagan, need love lives. They take matters into their own matchmaking hands and their efforts pay off. Soon their determined-to-stay-single parents find out just how hard it is to avoid two teenage cupids' arrows and to control their overheated hormones....

I hope you find Chance and Kylie's story as fun, sexy and heartwarming as I did. When you get a chance, please visit my Web site at www.brendajackson.net to view a special book trailer that introduces this story and the handsome Steele brothers.

Let the celebration begin,

Brenda Jackson

To Gerald Jackson, Sr., my husband and hero.

To my sons, Gerald and Brandon,
who constantly make me proud.

To my agent extraordinaire, Pattie Steele Perkins.

To my editor, Mavis Allen, who asked me
to be a part of the Kimani Romance line.

To my readers who have supported me
through 40 books.

Beloved, I wish above all things
that thou mayest prosper and be in good health,
even as thy soul prospereth.
—*3 John* 1:2

Prologue

"**M**y mom needs to get a life!"

With a sigh of both anger and frustration, fifteen-year-old Tiffany Hagan dropped down into the chair next to her friend, Marcus Steele.

"I thought you said that the reason you and your mom moved here to Charlotte a few months ago *was* for a better life," sixteen-year-old Marcus said after taking a huge bite of his hamburger as they sat in the school's cafeteria.

Tiffany rolled her eyes. "Yeah, that's what I thought, but now it seems that her idea of a better life is making mine miserable. Just because she got pregnant at sixteen doesn't mean I'd go out and do the same thing. Yeah right! I don't even have a boyfriend and if she keeps up her guard-dog mentality, I never will. She needs a life that doesn't revolve around me."

"Good luck in her getting one," Marcus said, taking a sip of his soda. "My dad is the same way, maybe even worse. He's so hell-bent on me making good grades and getting into an Ivy League college that I barely have time to breathe. If it weren't for my three uncles I probably wouldn't be playing football. Dad sees any extracurricular activities as a distraction."

Tiffany shook her head in disgust. "Parents! They're so controlling. Can't they see that they're smothering us?"

"Evidently not."

"I wish there was some way that I can shift my mom's attention off of me," Tiffany said, unwrapping her sandwich. "If only she had another interest, like a boyfriend or something. Then she could get all wrapped up in him and give me some breathing space. I don't remember her ever dating anyone."

After taking another bite of his hamburger, Marcus

said, "My dad has dated occasionally since my mom died seven years ago, and although I'm sure some of the women have tried, none of them holds his attention for long."

Tiffany laughed. "Then he better not ever meet my mom. One look at her and he'll be a goner for sure. I hate to brag but my mom is hot," she said proudly.

"Hey, my dad doesn't look too bad, either." Marcus grinned. "Maybe we ought to get them together since it seems that neither of them has a life," he added teasingly.

Tiffany was about to bite into her sandwich when Marcus' suggestion sank in. A huge smile curved her lips. "Marcus, that's it!"

He looked at her, baffled. "What's it?"

"My mom and your dad. Both are single, good-looking and desperately in need of something to occupy their time besides us. Just think of the possibilities."

Marcus began thinking. Moments later, he smiled. "Yeah," he agreed. "It just might work."

"It *would* work. Think about it. If we got them together, they would be so into each other that they wouldn't have time to drive us nuts."

"Yeah, but how can we get them together without them getting suspicious about anything?" he asked.

Tiffany smiled mischievously. "Oh, I bet I could think of something...."

Chapter 1

Less than a week later

Kylie Hagan regarded with keen interest the handsome specimen of a man dressed in a dark business suit, who had just walked into her florist shop. That was *so* unlike her. She couldn't recall the last time a member of the male species had grabbed her attention. Denzel Washington didn't count, since each and every time she saw him on the movie screen it was an automatic drool.

She continued watering her plants, thinking that

the woman he was about to buy flowers for was indeed very lucky. The good news was that he had selected her florist shop—she was the newbie in town, and Kylie needed all the business she could get, since she'd only been open for a couple of months. Business was good but she needed to come up with ways to make it even better.

Her heart jumped nervously when, instead of looking around at her vast selection of green plants and floral arrangements, he headed straight for the counter. Evidently he was a man who knew what he wanted and what he needed to woo his woman.

"May I help you?" she asked, thinking that with a face and physique like his, he probably didn't need much help at all. He stood tall, six-three at least, with a muscular build, a clean-shaven head, chocolate-brown eyes and skin tone of the richest cocoa, altogether a striking combination. The drool she usually reserved only for Denzel was beginning to make her mouth feel wet. As she continued to look at him, waiting for his response, she suddenly noticed that he wasn't smiling. In fact, he appeared downright annoyed.

"I'm here to see Kylie Hagan."

Kylie lifted her eyebrows and the smile on her face began fading at his rough and irritated tone of voice. What business did this man have with her? All her bills were current, which meant he couldn't be there to collect anything. And if he was a salesman, with his less than desirable attitude, she wouldn't be buying what-ever it was he was selling.

"I'm Kylie Hagan."

Surprise flickered in his drop-dead gorgeous eyes. "You're Kylie Hagan?"

"That's right and who are you?"

"Chance Steele."

The name didn't ring a bell, but then she had only recently moved to the area. "And what can I do for you, Mr. Steele?"

He stared at her for a moment, and then he said, "The only thing you can do for me, Ms. Hagan, is keep your daughter away from my son."

Kylie froze. The man's words were not what she had expected. For a long moment she stared back at him, wondering if she had misunderstood. But all it took was the deep scowl on his face to let her know she had not.

"Keep my daughter away from your son?" she repeated when she finally found her voice.

"Yes. I found this note yesterday that evidently dropped out of Marcus's backpack. They were planning on cutting school together on Friday," he said as he pulled a piece of paper out of the pocket of his jacket.

"What!" Kylie shrieked, grabbing the paper out of his hand.

"You heard me and you can read it for yourself," he said, crossing his arms over his chest.

Kylie read, then after the first few lines she wished she hadn't. Three emotions enveloped her: hurt, betrayal and anger. Tiffany had always promised that if she ever got serious about a boy that she would tell her. Granted, she and Tiffany hadn't been that close lately, but a promise was a promise.

"Now can you see why I want your daughter kept away from my son?"

Chance Steele's question sliced through Kylie's tormented mind and grated on her last nerve, deepening her anger. She came from behind the counter to stand directly in front of him. "Don't you dare place all the blame on Tiffany, Mr. Steele. If I read this note correctly, she was merely responding to a note your son had sent asking *her* to cut school. The nerve of him doing such a thing!"

"Look, Ms. Hagan, we can stand here all day and we won't agree who's to blame. But I think we will agree on the fact that your daughter and my son shouldn't even be thinking about cutting school. I have big plans for my son's future that include him attending college."

Kylie glared at him. "And you don't think I have those same plans for my daughter?" she snapped. "Tiffany is a good kid."

"So is Marcus," he snapped back.

Kylie breathed in deeply and closed her eyes in a concerted effort to calm down before a blood vessel burst in her head. They weren't getting anywhere biting each other's heads off.

"Ms. Hagan, are you all right?"

She slowly opened her eyes to focus on the man looming over her. Concern was evident in his gaze. "Yes, I'm fine."

"Look, I'm sorry I came barging in here like this," he said, the tone of his voice calmer, apologetic. "But after reading that note I got upset."

She nodded. "I can understand why. I'm pretty upset myself."

"Did you know our kids were hung up on each other?" he asked. She could tell that he was trying to maintain a composed demeanor.

"Mr. Steele, until you walked into my shop and dropped your son's name, I had no idea he even existed. Tiffany and I moved here a few months ago from New York State, right before the start of the new school year. I knew she had made some new friends but she's never mentioned anyone's name in particular."

"Okay, so as parents, what do you think we should do?" he asked.

His voice was drenched in wariness and Kylie could tell he was deeply bothered by all of this, but then he wasn't the only one. "The one thing we shouldn't do is demand that they not see each other. Telling them to stay away from each other will only make them want to see each other more. Teenagers will always deliberately do the opposite of what their parents want them to do. And once they start rebelling, it will be almost impossible to do anything."

She didn't have to tell him that she knew firsthand how that worked. Her parents had tried to keep her and Sam apart, which only made her want him more. The more she and Sam had sneaked around, the more risks they had taken until she had eventually gotten pregnant at sixteen…the same age Tiffany would be in about ten months.

"We have to do something. In confronting Marcus about that letter, I've thrown a monkey wrench into their plans for Friday. But how can we be sure this won't happen again?"

At the sound of Chance's voice, Kylie dragged

her thoughts back to the present. "I'll talk to Tiffany and, like I said, she's a good kid."

"Yes, but it appears that my son and your daughter are at the age where overactive hormones cancel out good sense. We need to do what we can to make sure those hormones stay under control."

"I fully agree."

He reached into his pocket and pulled out a business card. "This is how to reach me if you need me to do anything further on my end. I talked to Marcus but things didn't go well. I did the one thing you indicated I should not have done, which was demand that he stay away from Tiffany. I don't think I've ever seen him that angry or rebellious."

Kylie nodded as she took the card from him. She didn't want to think about her upcoming talk with Tiffany. "I appreciate you dropping by and bringing this to my attention."

"Like I said earlier, I apologize that my approach wasn't more subtle. But Marcus's last words to me this morning were that nobody would stop him from seeing Tiffany. I was furious and still riled up when I decided to come over here."

He sighed deeply and then added, "It's not easy raising a teenager these days."

"Don't I know it," Kylie said softly, feeling

terribly drained but knowing she would need all her strength when she confronted Tiffany after school.

"Well, I'd better be going."

"Again, thanks for coming by and letting me know what's going on."

He nodded. "There was no way I could *not* let you know, considering what they'd planned to do. Have a good day, Ms. Hagan."

As Kylie watched him walk out of her shop, she knew that as much as she wished it to be so, there was no way that this would be a good day.

The moment Chance got into his truck and closed the door, he leaned back against the seat and released a long sigh. If the daughter looked anything like the mother, he was in deep trouble. No wonder his usually smart son had begun acting downright stupid.

Kylie Hagan was definitely a beauty. He had noticed that fact the moment he had walked into the flower shop and headed straight toward the counter. When she had come from behind that same counter and he'd seen that she was wearing a pair of shorts and a T-shirt, he'd thought the outfit fit just right on her curvy, petite body and showed off her shapely legs too perfectly. Braided dark brown hair had been stylishly cut to accent her face. Her creamy chocolate skin complemented a pair of beautiful brown eyes, a perky nose and an incredibly feminine pair of lips.

How in the world could she be the mother of a fifteen-year-old when she looked barely older than twenty herself? She looked more like Tiffany's sister than her mother. Perhaps Tiffany had been adopted. There were a lot of questions circulating around in his mind, but the foremost was what the two of them could do about their kids who seemed hell-bent on starting a relationship that neither was ready for.

He understood Marcus's interest in girls—after all he was a Steele—and Chance could distinctly remem-ber when he was younger. He had fallen in love with Cyndi when he'd been just a few years older than Marcus, and had married her before his nineteenth birthday after she had gotten pregnant.

Pregnant.

He would never forget that day when Cyndi had come to him, a mere week before he was to leave for Yale University, to let him know she was having his baby. He had loved her so much he decided not to accept a full college scholarship and leave her alone. Instead, he had married her, gone to work at his father's manufacturing company and attended college at night. It hadn't been easy and it had taken

him almost six years to get a degree, but he and
Cyndi had made the best of it and he could look back
and honestly say that although there were hard years,
they had been happy ones.

And then the unthinkable happened. Cyndi had
noticed changes in a mole on the side of her neck, a
mole that was later determined to be cancerous. Even
after surgery and chemo treatments, four years later,
on the day Marcus should have been celebrating his
ninth birthday, they were in the cemetery putting to
rest the one woman who had meant the world to
Chance.

He straightened and started up his truck. Although
he would never think of marrying Cyndi as a
mistake, he couldn't help but remember her plans of
attending college; plans that had gotten thrown by
the wayside with her pregnancy. If he had it all to do
over, he would have been more responsible that night
when they had gotten carried away by the moment.

And then on top of everything else, he couldn't
forget the promise he had made to Cyndi on her
deathbed; a promise that he would make sure that
their son got to do everything they hadn't done, and
take advantage of every opportunity offered to him,
which included one day attending a university that
would give him the best education.

That was the reason he was driven to make sure Marcus did well in school. Of course it was Chance's hope for him to one day join the family business, the Steele Corporation, but if Marcus wanted to do something else after finishing college, then he could do so with Chance's blessings.

As he began backing out of the parking lot, he contemplated the emergence of Tiffany Hagan in Marcus's life. He didn't think his son's interest in the girl was going to fade away anytime soon, regardless of what kind of talk Kylie Hagan had with her daughter. That meant Chance needed to have a "Plan B" ready. Under no circumstances would he let Marcus succumb to teen lust and ruin the life he and Cyndi always wanted for him.

His thoughts shifted to Tiffany's mother again, and he felt lust invading his own body. The difference was he was a man and he could handle it.

At least he hoped he could.

After reading the note, Helena Spears glanced up at the woman who'd been her best friend since high school. "Are you sure Tiffy wrote this, Kylie?"

The two of them had met for lunch and were sitting at a table in the back of the restaurant. Kylie shook her head. Leave it to Lena to try to wiggle her goddaughter out of any kind of trouble. "Of course I'm sure. I can recognize Tiffany's handwriting when I see it and so can you. Those curls at the end of certain letters give her away and you know it."

Lena shrugged as she handed the note back to Kylie. "Well, the only thing I have to say in defense of my godchild is that if Marcus looks anything like his daddy, then I can see why Tiffy fell for him."

Kylie didn't want to admit that she'd thought the same thing. "You know Chance Steele?"

"Oh, yeah. There are few people living in Charlotte who don't know the Steele brothers. They own a huge manufacturing company, the Steele Corporation. There are four of them who were born and raised here. They're not transplants like rest of us, and they are very successful, as well as handsome. Chance is the CEO and his brothers have key positions in the corporation. There are also three female cousins, one of which works in the PR Department. The other two chose careers outside of the company, but all three are members of the board of direc-tors."

Lena took a sip of her drink before continuing. "Chance is the oldest and the one I see most often with my charity work. He's a big supporter of the American Cancer Society. His wife died of cancer around seven years ago."

Kylie, who had been putting the note back in her purse, suddenly lifted her head. "He's a widower?"

"Yes, and from what I understand, he's doing a good job raising his son."

Kylie frowned. "Not if his son is enticing girls to cut school with him."

Lena laughed. "Oh, come on, Kylie. You were young once."

"I remember. And that's what I'm afraid of," she said, meeting Lena's gaze with a concerned expression. "You recall how I was all into Sam. I thought I was madly in love. It was like my day wasn't complete until I saw his face. I was obsessed."

Lena shook her head. "Yeah, you did have it bad. You thought you were in love, and nobody could tell you differently."

"And you saw what happened to me. One day of acting irresponsibly changed my entire life. I was pregnant on my sixteenth birthday."

And rejected at sixteen as well.

She would never forget the day Sam told her that he wanted no part of her or the baby, and that he would get his parents to give her money for an abortion, but that was about all she would ever get from him. He intended to go to college on a football scholarship and under no circumstances would he let her mess up his future with a baby he didn't want. He agreed with his parents that there was no sense in him throwing away a promising career in pro football because of one foolish mistake. So instead of hanging around and doing the right thing, he had split the first chance he got. Even now she could count on one hand the number of times Tiffany had seen her father. Sam did get the football career in the NFL that he'd wanted, at least for a short while before an injury ended things. Now he was living in California, married with a family, and rarely had time for his daughter.

Emotions tightened her throat as she remembered that time she had gotten pregnant. She had hurt her parents something awful. And disappointed them as well. They had had so many high hopes for her, their only child, including her attending college at their alma mater, Southern University.

She had eventually gotten a college degree but that was only after years of struggling as a single parent and trying to make a life for her and Tiffany. And now to think that her daughter could possibly be traveling down the same path was unacceptable.

"Yes, I did see what happened to you, but look how much you've accomplished since then, Kylie," Lena said. "The only thing you didn't do was allow another man into your life because of Sam's rejection, and I think you were wrong for turning away what I knew were some good men. You never gave yourself the chance for happiness with someone else after Sam. I tried to tell you how arrogant and selfish he was but you wouldn't listen."

Kylie sighed. No, she hadn't wanted to hear anything negative about Sam. She had been too much in love to see his faults and refused to let anyone else talk about them, either. A sickening sensation swelled in her stomach at the thought that history was about to repeat itself with her child. "That's why I can't let Tiffany make the same mistake I did, Lena."

"Don't you think you and Chance might be over-reacting just a little? It's not like Tiffy and Marcus planned to cut the entire day of school. They were skipping the last two classes to go somewhere, probably to the mall," Lena pointed out.

"And that's supposed to be okay?" Kylie's nerves were screaming in frustration and anger each and every time she thought about what her daughter had planned on doing. She remembered when she had cut school with Sam. Instead of going to the movies like the two of them planned, he had taken her to his house, where they had spent the entire day in his bedroom doing things they shouldn't have been doing and things neither of them had been prepared for. But all she could think about was that Sam Miller, the star player on the Richardson High School football team, was in love with her. Or so she'd thought. Silly her.

"You need to calm down before you talk to Tiff, Kylie. I understand you're upset, but your anger won't help. You know how headstrong she is. She's just like you when you were her age."

Kylie sighed deeply. Again that was the last thing she wanted to hear. "She broke her promise to me, Lena. We've had a lot of talks. She had promised me that she would let me know when she was interested in boys."

"And had she come and told you about Marcus, then what? Would you have given her your blessings or locked her up for the rest of her life? Girls like boys, Kylie. That's natural. And you've had so many talks with Tiffy that she probably knows your speech by heart. Has it ever occurred to you that maybe you're laying things on a little too thick? Tiffy is a good kid, yet you're judging her by the way you lived your life, by your own past mistakes. It's important to you that she 'be good' because you don't think that you were."

Kylie's eyes began filling with tears. "I only want what's best for her, Lena. I made a foolish and stupid mistake once and I'll do anything within my power to keep her from making the same one."

Lena got up, came around the table and hugged her friend. "I know. Tiffy is going to be fine. I'll be here to help you anyway that I can. You know that. I just don't want you to build this brick wall between you and her. That same kind of wall your mother built with you."

Kylie wiped away a tear from her cheek. Although she and her mother had a fairly decent relationship now, Kylie would never forget when Olivia Hagan had let down her only daughter by upholding her belief that by getting pregnant out of wedlock, Kylie had committed the worst possible sin.

"I'll never let that happen," Kylie vowed quietly.

Chapter 2

"That's the crisis you called this meeting for?" Sebastian Steele asked, turning away from the window and looking across the office at his brother with both amazement and amusement on his face.

Chance glared first at Sebastian, and then at his other two brothers, Morgan and Donovan. They were sitting in front of his desk and looking at him with the same expressions. "Your nephew is putting a pretty face before his studies and that doesn't add up to a crisis to any of you?"

When all three chimed the word "no" simultaneously, Chance knew talking to them had been a waste of his time.

At the age of thirty-six, Chance was the oldest of the group. Next was Sebastian, fondly called Bas, who was thirty-four. Morgan was thirty-two, and Donovan was thirty. Of the four, Chance was the only one who had ever been married. Bas was presently engaged, but the other two claimed they enjoyed their bachelor status too much to settle down anytime soon.

"Look, Chance," Morgan said as he stood up. "It's normal for boys Marcus's age to like girls. So what's the problem?"

Chance rolled his eyes heavenward. "The problem is that the girl is only fifteen and they were planning to cut school together and—"

"No," Sebastian interrupted. "They planned to cut a couple of classes, not school. There is a difference."

"And he of all people should know," Donovan said, grinning. "Considering the number of times he used to play hooky. I understand they still have a desk in Mr. Potter's math class that says, 'Sebastian Steele never sat here.'"

"I don't find any of this amusing," Chance said.

Morgan wiped the grin off his face. "Then maybe you should, before you alienate your son."

"How about chilling here, Chance," Sebastian interjected. "You act as if Marcus committed some god-awful sin. We know the promise you made to Cyndi, but there is more to life for a teenager than hitting the books. He's a good kid. He makes good grades. Marcus is going to go to college in a couple of years, we all know that. One girl isn't going to stop him."

"You haven't seen this girl."

Morgan raised a brow. "Have you?"

"No, but I've seen her mother, and if the daughter looks anything like the mother then I'm in trouble."

"I still think you're blowing things out of proportion," Morgan countered. "If you make a big deal out of it, Marcus will rebel. You remember what happened last year when you didn't want him to play football."

Yes, Chance did remember, although he wished he could forget. He rubbed his hand down his face. Regardless of what his brothers said, he needed to talk to Marcus again. He didn't have any problems with his son being interested in girls, he just didn't want Marcus losing his head over one this soon.

Kylie was waiting in the living room the moment Tiffany walked through the door. She took one look at her daughter's expression and realized Tiffany knew the conversation that was about to take place. Kylie tried not to show her anger, as well as a few other emotions, when she said, "We need to talk."

Tiffany met her mother's stare. "Look, Mom, I know what you're going to say and I don't think I did anything wrong."

So much for not showing her anger, Kylie thought. "How can you say that? You planned to cut classes with a boy and you don't consider that wrong?"

Tiffany rolled her eyes. "My last two classes of the day are boring anyway, so we—"

"Boring? I don't care how boring they are, you're supposed to be in them and you *will* be in them anytime that bell sounds. Understood?"

Tiffany glared at her. "Yes, I understand."

Kylie nodded. "Now, about Marcus Steele."

Tiffany straightened her spine and immediately went on the defensive. "What about Marcus?"

"Why didn't you tell me about him?"

"Why? So you could find some reason for me not to like him, Mom? Well, it won't work because I do like him. You're the one who wanted to leave Buffalo and move here. And I'm the one who was forced to go to another school and make new friends. Not all of the kids at school like me. They say I talk funny. Marcus has been nice to me. Extremely nice. He asked me to be his girlfriend and I said yes."

"You're not old enough to have a boyfriend, Tiffany."

"That's your rule, Mom."

"And one you will abide by, young lady."

"Why? Because you think I'll get pregnant like you did? That's not fair."

"It's not about that, Tiffany. It's about such things as keeping your reputation intact and not getting involved in anything you aren't ready for."

"It *is* about what happened to you when you were sixteen, Mom. And how do you know what I am or am not ready for? You want to shelter me and you can't. You've talked to me, but the choice of what I do is ultimately mine."

"No, it's not," Kylie bit out. "As long as you're living under my roof, I make the rules and you will abide by them."

"I can't, Mom. I care too much for Marcus and we have news for you and Mr. Steele. We are madly in love!" she almost shouted. "And nothing either of you say is going to make us not be together, whether it's at school or someplace else."

"What's that supposed to mean?"

"It means," Tiffany said stalking off to her room, "that I don't want to talk anymore."

Chance leaped to his feet. The sound of his chair crashing to the floor echoed loudly in the kitchen. "What do you mean you might not go to college but stay in Charlotte to be closer to Tiffany Hagan?" he shouted. His anger had clearly reached the boiling point.

"There's no reason to get upset, Dad. What's the big deal if I decided to hang around here and go to college? One university is just as good as another."

Chance rubbed his hand down his face, trying to fight for composure, and quickly decided to use another approach. "Marcus," he said calmly, "I'm sure Tiffany Hagan is a nice girl, but you're only sixteen. In another couple of years you'll finish high school and go to college where you will meet plenty of other nice girls. You have such a bright future ahead of you. I'd hate to see you get too serious about any girl now."

A stubborn expression settled on Marcus's face. "She's not just any girl, Dad. Tiffany is the girl I plan to marry one day."

"Marry!" Chance nearly swallowed the word in

shock. "How did marriage get into the picture? You're only sixteen! I know you think you really care for this girl and—"

"It's more than that, Dad, and the sooner you and Tiffany's mother realize it, the better. Tiffany and I are madly in love and we want to be together forever. There's nothing either of you can say or do to stop us, so you may as well accept it."

"Like hell I will."

"I'm sorry to hear that," Marcus said as he walked out of the kitchen toward his bedroom.

Total shock kept Chance from going after his son and wringing his neck.

Kylie paced the floor. Her nerves were stretched to the breaking point. Tiffany hadn't come out of her room yet, which was probably the best thing.

Love!

At fifteen her daughter thought she was in love. Madly in love at that! Kylie swallowed a thickness in her throat when she realized how her mother must have felt sixteen years ago, dealing with her when she'd been obsessed with Sam Miller.

She paused when she heard the phone ring and quickly crossed the room to pick it up, thinking it was probably Lena checking to see how things with Tiffany had gone. "Hello."

"We need to talk, Ms. Hagan."

Kylie blinked at the sound of the ultra sexy male voice. It didn't take a rocket scientist to figure out who the caller was, or to know he'd evidently had had another talk with his son. She sighed. Yes, they did need to talk. "You name the place and I'll be there."

"All right." After a quiet pause, he said. "They *think* they're in love. Madly in love."

Kylie shook her head. "So I heard. Louder than I really cared to, in fact."

"Same here. Do you know where the Racetrack Café is?"

"Yes."

"Can you meet me there around noon tomorrow?"

Considering what was going on with Tiffany and his son, she really didn't have a choice. Hopefully, together they could devise a way to stop the young couple before they got into more trouble than they could handle. "Yes, I can meet you there."

"Fine, I'll see you then."

Chance arrived at the restaurant early to make sure they got a table. Jointly owned by several race car drivers on the NASCAR circuit, the Racetrack Café was a popular eatery in town. He hadn't been seated more than five minutes when he glanced over at the entrance to see Kylie Hagan walk in.

He had hoped his mental picture of her from yesterday had been wrong, but it hadn't. Kylie Hagan was an attractive woman. Every man in the place apparently thought so, too, judging by the looks they gave her. Not for the first time he wondered about her age and how someone who looked so young could have a fifteen-year-old daughter.

He watched her glance around before she spotted him. There wasn't even a hint of a smile on her face as she walked toward him. But, he quickly decided, it didn't matter. Smiling or not, she looked gorgeous dressed in a pair of black slacks and a blue pullover sweater. And those same curves that he'd convinced himself had to be a figment of his imagination made her slacks a perfect fit for her body. Even her walk was mesmerizing and sexy.

When she got closer, he saw the wariness around her eyes, which led him to believe that she'd probably gone a round or two with her daughter sometime during that day, as he'd done with Marcus. He wondered if the discussion had been about the "his and hers" tattoos Marcus had indicated he and Tiffany were thinking about getting.

Chance stood when she reached the table. "Ms. Hagan."

"Mr. Steele."

He thought they were overdoing the formality, but felt it was best to keep things that way for now. After all, this was nothing more than a business meeting, and the only item on the agenda was a discussion about their children.

After they had taken their seats, he asked, "Would you like to order anything? They have the best hamburgers and French fries in town."

A small smile touched Kylie's lips. "So I've heard. But no, I'm fine, you go ahead and order something if you'd like. It's just that my most recent conversation with Tiffany has killed my appetite."

Chance heard the quiver in her voice and recalled his own conversation with Marcus that morning before he'd left for school. "I take it Tiffany told you about the tattoo."

He watched her nostrils flare as she drew in a silent breath. "Yes, she told me. Matching lovebirds on their tummies right above their navels, I understand."

"That's my understanding as well." A soft chuckle erupted from his throat. There was a cloud hanging over his head that refused to go away and he had to find amusement anywhere he could to keep his sanity. But he had to believe this was just one part of parenthood that he would get through, and for some reason it was important to him for Kylie Hagan to believe that as well.

"Things are going to be all right, Ms. Hagan," he said soothingly. "That's why we're meeting today, to make sure of it." He flashed her a smile.

She glanced up and met his gaze. "I want to believe that," she said quietly. "Under the circumstances I think we should forgo formality. Please call me Kylie."

"Okay, and I'm Chance." After a pause he said, "Kylie, I want you to believe things will work out. We have to think positively that we'll get through this particular episode in our children's lives. We have good kids—they're just a little headstrong and stubborn. But I believe with some parental guidance they'll be fine."

"I hope so. Otherwise if they continue with the route they're going, they're bound to make a mistake."

Chance raised a brow. "By mistake you mean...?"

"Taking their relationship to a level they aren't ready for, Chance."

He liked the way his name easily flowed from her lips. "I take it you mean sex."

"Yes, that's precisely what I'm talking about. Over the years, I've had the mother-daughter talks with Tiffany, but when teenagers are in love, or think they're in love, they believe that sex is just another way to show how much they care."

They paused in their conversation when a waitress came to give Chance his beer, hand them menus and fill their water glasses.

"And you think that's going to be on their minds?" he asked.

"Of course. Raging teenage hormones are the worst kind."

He picked up his glass to take a sip of beer. "Are they?"

"Yes, trust me, I know. I had Tiffany when I was sixteen."

Chance's glass stopped midway to his lips. His mouth opened in surprise. "Sixteen?"

"Yes. So I hope you can understand why I'm upset with all of this. I don't want Tiffany to make the same mistake I made as a teenager."

Chance nodded. That explained the reason Kylie didn't look old enough to have a fifteen-year-old daughter. That meant she was around thirty-one, but still she didn't look a day over twenty-five. "Did you and Tiffany's father get married?"

Her laugh was bitter. "Are you kidding? He had to make a choice between me and a football scholarship to Hampton University. He chose college."

"I didn't."

Kylie glanced up from studying her water glass. "You didn't what?"

"I was faced with the same decision as Tiffany's father. My girlfriend, Marcus's mother, got pregnant when we were seniors in high school. We were both eighteen and had plans for college. We acknowledged our mistake and felt that no matter what, we loved each other and loved the child we had made. Instead of going to college, we got married, remained here in Charlotte and made the best of things. I later went to college at night. My wife died of cancer when Marcus was nine."

Chance finished his beer. A part of him regretted that the man who had gotten Kylie pregnant hadn't done the responsible thing. "It must have been hard for you, pregnant at sixteen," he said.

"It was." He could tell by the way her lips were quivering their conversation was bringing back painful memories for her. "I disappointed my parents tremendously, embarrassed them. When it was determined that the father didn't want me or his child as part of his future, my parents tried talking me into giving up my baby for adoption, but I refused. That caused friction between us the entire nine months. Things got so bad at home that I had to go live with my best friend and her mother the last couple months of my pregnancy."

After taking a sip of water, she said, "The day the nurse brought Tiffany to me for the first time after I'd given birth to her, I gazed down at my beautiful daughter and knew I had made the right decision, no matter how my parents felt."

"Did they eventually come around to your way of thinking?"

"Years later when they realized they were denying themselves the chance to get to know their grand-daughter. But at first they wanted me to know what a mistake I'd made in keeping her. They'd intended to teach me a lesson. I couldn't move back home so I continued to live with my friend's family until I was able to get an apartment at seventeen. I finished high school at night while working at a grocery store as a cashier during the day. My best friend, who also became Tiffany's godmother, kept her at night so I could finish school. It was hard but I was determined to make it work. After high school, I went to college and I struggled for years as a single parent before I finally earned a degree. I got a management position and later purchased a modest home for me and Tiffany."

"What made you decide to move here?"

"The company where I worked as a supervisor decided to downsize. My position was no longer needed so they gave me a pretty nice severance package. Instead of seeing losing my job as the end of the world, I decided to turn it into an opportunity to do something I'd always wanted to do."

"Open up a florist shop?"

"Yes. The reason I decided on Charlotte was that Lena had moved here after college and I liked the area the couple of times I'd come to visit her."

"Lena?"

"Helena Spears, my best friend from high school."

Chance smiled. "Helena Spears? I've met her on several occasions. She's a Realtor in town and is very active with the Cancer Society. I think her father died of the disease some years ago."

"He did, when Lena was fourteen. In recent years her mother has taken ill. I admire Lena for taking on the responsibility of her mother's care the way she has."

Kylie leaned back in her chair. "So knowing my

history, Chance, I hope you can understand why I don't want Tiffany to make the same mistakes I did. I don't have anything against your son personally. I'm sure he's a fine young man. I just don't think he and Tiffany are ready for any sort of a relationship just yet."

"And I totally agree. So what do you think we should do?"

"I think we should meet with them, tell them our feelings, let them know we understand how they feel, or how they think they feel, since we were young once. But we should try to do whatever we can to slow down things between them. They're moving too fast. One day I didn't even know Marcus existed and now my daughter is claiming to be madly in love with him."

When the waitress came back to take their order, Chance glanced over at Kylie. "You're still not hungry?"

Kylie smiled. "Yes, in fact I think I'm going to try a hamburger and fries."

Chance returned her smile. "I think I will, too."

"I'm glad we had our little talk," Chance said as he walked Kylie to her car an hour or so later.

"So am I," she said honestly, although the whole

time she'd sat across from him she'd had to fight back her drool. She was amazed at the thoughts that had crept into her mind. Thoughts of how Chance Steele had to have one of the sexiest mouths she'd ever seen. And the type of physique that drew feminine attention. Watching him eat had been quite an ordeal. She'd had to fight the urge to squirm in her seat each time he bit into his hamburger. Her attraction to him was truly bizarre, considering the real problem was finding a way to keep their kids in line.

But she would be crazy not to acknowledge that she was drawn to him in a way she hadn't been drawn to a man in years. Sexual longings were something she hadn't had to deal with for quite some time. Being in Chance's company she had been reminded of just how long it had been.

"So we've decided that I'm to bring Marcus over to your place for Sunday dinner so the four of us can sit down and talk," he said when they reached her car.

"Yes, that's the plan."

"And I think it's a good one. We need to talk to them, but even more importantly, we need to let them talk to us. And no matter what, we're going to have to keep our cool, even when we'd like nothing better than to ring their little necks. The situation we're dealing with calls for strategy and tact, not anger."

She tilted her head up and looked at him. "Strategy and tact I can handle, but it's going to be hard keeping my anger in check," she said, thinking of the conversation she'd had with Tiffany that morning before the girl had left for school. Her daughter was intent on being stubborn, no matter what.

"We'll not only get through it, we'll succeed," Chance said.

Kylie knew he was trying to alleviate some of her worries and she appreciated it. "Okay, then I'll see you and Marcus on Sunday. I'm looking forward to meeting him."

"And I'm looking forward to meeting Tiffany as well." As he held the car door for her he shook his head and laughed. "Matching lovebird tattoos. Have you ever heard of anything so ridiculous?"

Chance drew Kylie into his amusement. "No, and what's really crazy is that Tiffany is petrified of needles."

"Well, it's been said that love makes you do foolish things."

Later that night Chance swore as he got out of bed. For the first time in eight years, a woman other than his wife had invaded his dreams. Every time he'd closed his eyes, he'd seen Kylie Hagan's face.

It seemed as if he couldn't keep his mind from dredging up memories of her. First there was her appearance yesterday when a T-shirt and a pair of shorts covered her shapely body. And today, at the café, the slacks and sweater she'd been wearing had made him appreciate the fact that he was a male.

And then there were the times she would do something as simple as drink water from her glass. He couldn't help but watch the long, smooth column of her throat as water passed down it. He had wanted to kiss every inch of her neck and had wondered how it would feel for her to grip him the way she was gripping her glass.

Chance dragged a hand down his face thinking it had been a long time for him. Way too long. Sexual cravings were something he'd barely had to deal with, but now he was having several sharp attacks. In addition to the lust he was feeling for her, he also felt a deep sense of admiration.

She had given birth to a child at sixteen, hadn't given in to her parents' demand that she give the child up for adoption, and had struggled the past fifteen years as a single parent who'd gotten a college education and had provided for herself and her daughter. He considered what she'd done a success story. What he really appreciated was the fact that her past experiences enabled her to foresee what could be a potentially dangerous situation for Tiffany and Marcus. It was clear as glass that she didn't want them to make the same mistake she'd made.

As he left the bedroom and headed for the kitchen, he thought about his own situation with Cyndi. They had been blessed in that both sets of parents had been supportive of their decision to keep their child and marry. And when Marcus was born, there was no doubt in Chance's mind that Cyndi's parents, as well as his own, loved their first grandchild unconditionally. His heart went out to both Kylie and Tiffany when he thought about what they had been denied.

His pulse began racing when he thought about dinner at Kylie's place on Sunday when he would be seeing her again. That was one dinner engagement that he was looking forward to.

Kylie awoke with a start, finding that she was drenched in sweat…or heat, since what had awakened her was an erotic dream.

Chance Steele had kissed her, touched her, made love to her. At first she had moaned in protest but then they'd become moans of pleasure. But at the exact moment he was about to do away with all the mind-blowing foreplay and enter her body to take total possession, she had awakened.

She pulled herself into a sitting position and struggled to calm her ragged breath. Perspiration cloaked her body, a sign of just how long she had been in denial. For a brief moment, everything had seemed real, including the way his skin felt beneath her palms, how thick and solid his muscles were against her body and just how good those same muscles felt melding into hers.

With a deep sigh of disgust, she threw the covers back and got out of bed. Why, after fifteen years, did she finally become attracted to a man who just happened to the be the father of the boy who could become her worst nightmare? On the way to the bathroom, she inwardly cursed for finding Chance so damn handsome.

As she turned on the shower and began stripping out of her damp nightclothes, she thought about how her life had been over the past fifteen years. Sam was the first and only man she had slept with. Once Tiffany had been born, her precious little girl had become the most important thing to her, her very reason for existing, and the years that followed had been busy ones as a single parent. Although a number of men had shown interest, a relationship with any of them had taken a backseat. It was either bad timing or a lack of desire on her part to share herself with anyone other than Tiffany. In essence, she had placed her needs aside to take care of the needs of her child.

But now it seemed that those needs were catching up with her. Something sharp, unexpected and mind-blowingly stimulating was taking its toll. For years she had been able to keep those urges under control, but now it seemed a losing battle. It was as if her body was saying, *I won't let you deny me any longer.*

As she stepped into the shower and stood beneath the spray of water, she knew that she was in deep trouble. Not only did she have to deal with the situation going on with Tiffany and Marcus, but she had to deal with her own attraction to Chance. It was sheer foolishness to become this enamored with a man she had only met a couple of days ago, and the very thought that she had gone so far as to dream about him making love to her was totally unacceptable.

No matter how intense the sexual longings invading her body, she had to get a grip. And more than anything, she had to remember that men couldn't be depended on to always do the right thing. Sam had proven that to her in a big way, and so had

her father. He had let her down when he'd meekly
gone along with her mother's treatment of her when
she'd gotten pregnant.

Moments later when she stepped out of the
shower, dried off and donned a fresh nightgown, she
had to concede that the water hadn't washed any
thoughts of Chance from her mind. She had a feeling
that even when she went back to bed she wouldn't
experience anything close to a peaceful sleep.

Chapter 3

"You actually invited Marcus and his father for dinner on Sunday!"

Kylie lifted a brow as she washed her hands in the kitchen sink. Surprised at the excitement she heard in her daughter's voice, she turned to meet her gaze. "I take it that you don't have a problem with it."

The enthusiasm in Tiffany's voice dropped a degree when she shrugged her shoulders and said, "No, why should I? Just as long as you and Mr. Steele aren't going to try and break us up, because it won't happen. Marcus and I are—"

"Madly in love," Kylie rushed in to finish, stifling her anger as she dried her hands. "I know." If she heard her daughter exclaim the depth of her love for Marcus Steele one more time she would scream.

"I thought it would be a good idea for me to finally meet Marcus, considering how you feel about him," Kylie said.

"Why is Mr. Steele coming?"

"Because he's Marcus's father and, like me, he wants what's best for his child."

"Oh, then, he won't have to worry about a thing because I am the best."

Kylie rolled her eyes thinking her daughter was getting conceited lately—another of Sam's traits rearing its ugly head.

"So the two of you have been talking a lot?"

Kylie frowned as she began making the pancakes for breakfast. "The two of who?"

"You and Mr. Steele."

"More than we've wanted to, I'm sure," Kylie said with forced calmness. The last thing her daughter needed to know was just what an impact Chance Steele was having on her. Just as she'd figured last night, she hadn't been able to go back to sleep without visions of him dancing around in her head.

"How does he look?"

Many of the descriptive words that came to mind she couldn't possibly share with her daughter. "He's handsome, so I take it that Marcus is handsome, too."

Tiffany beamed. "Yes, of course." Then seconds later she said, "I heard Mr. Steele is nice."

Kylie expelled a deep breath. "I don't know him well enough to form an opinion but I have no reason to think that he's not." Although she pretended nonchalance, she couldn't stop herself from glancing over at Tiffany and asking, "Who told you he was nice?"

"Marcus. He thinks the world of his father."

Kylie's first reaction at hearing that statement was to ask why, if Marcus thought the world of his dad, he was causing Chance so much grief.

"He doesn't date much."

"Who?"

"Mr. Steele."

With his good looks and fine body, Kylie found that hard to believe. "Don't you think you need to start getting dressed for school?" she prompted, not wanting to discuss Chance any longer.

Tiffany nodded. "I'll be back in time for pancakes," she said as she rushed out of the kitchen.

When she was gone, Kylie leaned against the

counter wondering why Chance had dominated their conversation. Was there a possibility that Tiffany was nervous about meeting Marcus's father? She couldn't help but remember the first time Sam had taken her to meet his parents. They hadn't been impressed with her and hadn't wasted any time letting her and Sam know they thought the two of them were too young to be involved.

Too bad she hadn't taken the Millers's opinion seriously. How differently things would have turned out if she had. But then she could never regret having Tiffany in her life, even now when her daughter was determined to make her hair gray early.

So, she thought as she pulled the orange juice out of the refrigerator, Chance didn't date often. Rather interesting…

Chance leaned back in the chair and stared out his office window. Instead of reading the report from the research-and-development department, he was sitting at his desk thinking of a reason to call Kylie Hagan. After that dream last night, he had awoken obsessed with hearing her voice.

Gut-twisting emotions clawed through him. It was bad enough that his son was totally besotted with the daughter, now it seemed he was becoming obsessed with the mother. He hadn't even managed to brush his teeth this morning without Kylie consuming his thoughts. He gritted those same teeth, not liking the position he was in one damn bit.

It wasn't as if he hadn't dated since Cyndi's death. But he quickly admitted that Kylie was different from any woman he'd taken out. She had a strong, independent nature that he admired. She had raised her child alone and when times had gotten tough with the downsizing of her job, she had made what she'd felt were the best decisions for the both of them. Even considering all of that, he still wondered what about her had not only grabbed his attention but was holding it tight. Could it be that now that he was getting older with a son who would be leaving for college in a couple of years, the thought of being alone scared him? Of course, he had his brothers, but they had their own lives.

Sebastian was the corporation's problem solver and troubleshooter. The Steele Corporation was more than just a company to Bas; it was his lifeline. Bas had been the last brother to join the company, and of the four, he had been the one to give their parents the most grief while growing up. Cutting school on a regular basis had been minor considering the other things he'd done. His reputation for getting into mischief was legendary. Trouble had seemed to find Bas, even when he wasn't looking for it. His engagement had mystified his brothers since he was the last Steele anyone would have thought would want to tie the knot.

Then there was Morgan, who headed R & D. Although he dated, everyone teased Morgan about holding out for the perfect woman. So far he hadn't found a woman who qualified for the role, although he was convinced one existed.

Last but not least was Donovan, who women claimed could seduce them with his voice alone. The youngest of the Steele brothers headed product administration, but unlike Bas, who was married to the corporation, Donovan always managed to carve out some play time.

"It doesn't look like you're busy, big brother, so I'll just come in."

Chance turned his head and watched as Bas entered his office. He sat up, a little surprised that anyone, including his brother, had made it past his secretary without being announced. "Where's Joanna?" he asked. It was a rare occurrence for Joanna Cabot to leave her post without advising him.

Bas smiled. "Just where is your mind today, Chance? Have you forgotten that Robert Parker is retiring and today's his last day in sales? We were all at the celebration downstairs and wondering where you were. I made an excuse for you by telling everyone you probably had gotten detained on an important call."

Chance muttered a low curse. He had forgotten about Robert's retirement party. Robert had been part of the Steele Corporation when their father, Lester Steele, had run things. Now their retired parents were living the life in the Keys, doing all the things they'd always dreamed of doing, and had left the family business in the hands of their capable sons and niece.

"Yes, I'd forgotten about it."

Bas leaned against the closed door. "Umm, and you were just talking about it yesterday, which makes me wonder what's weighing so heavily on your mind."

Chance stood and quickly slipped into his suit jacket. "Trust me, you don't want to know."

Bas scowled. "You aren't losing sleep over that Marcus affair, are you? You are chilling like we told you to do, right?"

Chance decided not to tell Bas that the Marcus affair had conveniently become his own personal affair, thanks to Tiffany Hagan's mother. "Yes, I'm chilling."

Bas laughed. "You wouldn't know how to chill if your life depended on it."

Chance rolled his eyes, grinning. "Look who's talking."

It was a couple of hours later that Chance arrived back in his office. A part of him was still obsessed with hearing Kylie's voice. Deciding not to fight it any longer, he pulled out his wallet to find the business card she had given him the other day at the café. He picked up the phone, then put it back down. Damn, he wanted to do more than talk to her. He wanted to see her.

He reached for the phone and punched in the number to connect with his secretary. "Ms. Cabot, I'm leaving early today. If an emergency comes up you can reach me on my cell phone."

Strategy and tact were the methods he'd mentioned to Kylie for bringing their children around. Little did she know he was about to apply that same technique on her.

Kylie turned at the sound of the shop door opening with a smile of greeting on her lips. The smile quickly faded when she saw it was the one man who had invaded her dreams last night.

She took a calming breath, remembering her reaction the first time she'd seen him when he'd walked through her door two days ago. Nothing had changed. Dressed in another power-house business suit, he looked drop-dead gorgeous.

She tried not to stare at him like a love-struck teenager, but found she was helpless in doing so. Chance Steele wasn't just any man. He was the one man who had started her blood circulating again in some very intimate places. He was definitely a man who was the very epitome of everything male.

"Hi," she said, deciding to break the silence when they just stood there staring at each other.

"Hi." He then glanced around. "You're not busy."

"No, the lunch crowd has come and gone."

"Oh. Would you like to go out?"

She raised a brow. "Out where?"

"To lunch."

Surprise flickered in the depths of Kylie's dark eyes. "To lunch?"

"Yes," he said, giving her a smile that made her stomach clench. "Would you go to lunch with me?"

"Why? Do we need to talk about the kids again?"

"No."

That single word sent her mind into a spin. He

wanted to take her out but not to talk about the kids. Then what on earth would they talk about?

Chance must have seen the question in her eyes because he said, "I discovered something very important yesterday at the café, Kylie."

"What?"

"I enjoyed your company a lot. A whole lot." Then as an afterthought, he added, "I don't date often."

His confession was the same as Tiffany had said that very morning. Although she knew it probably wasn't good manners, Kylie couldn't help asking, "Why?"

He shrugged. "For a number of reasons but I can probably sum it up in one rationale."

"Which is?"

"Lack of interest."

Kylie knew all about lack of interest. She'd been dealing with it for over fifteen years. She hadn't wanted the drama of getting into a hot and heavy relationship with someone, nor had she wanted to expose Tiffany to the drama, either. "Oh, I see."

"Do you?"

Nervously, Kylie stared down at her hands, confused by a lot of questions, the main one being why she was more attracted to Chance than any other man. She lifted her head. "Then maybe I don't see after all."

Her heart began racing when he started crossing the room. When he came to a stop directly in front of her, he placed his finger under her chin, lifting her gaze to meet his. "In that case, for us to go to lunch together is a rather good idea."

She was warmed by his touch. "Why would you think that?"

"Because it would make things easier for us on Sunday if we were honest with ourselves about a few things now."

Kylie's eyes clung to his, knowing he was right. There was no need to play dumb. There was something happening between them that she didn't need or want, but it was happening anyway. And they needed to get it out in the open, talk about it and put a stop to it before it went any further. How could they help their kids battle lust when they'd found themselves in the same boat?

She drew in a deep breath. "All right, if you'll give me a second, I need to close up and put the Out to Lunch sign on the door."

He nodded. "Take your time. I'm not going anywhere."

Chance stood to the side while Kylie went about

closing her shop. His eyes roamed over her with more than mild intensity. For some reason, today she looked even younger than she had the other days. She was wearing shorts and a top again, and he thought her legs were just as shapely as he remembered and her body just as curvy.

He couldn't help the desire that quickly escalated to extreme hunger and hit him in the gut. For one intense moment, he felt a burning desire to walk across the room and take her mouth with his. The need to taste her was driving him insane.

"I'm ready."

He blinked, realizing she had spoken. He inhaled a calming breath and fought for composure. He was ready, too, but doubted they were ready for the same thing.

"One of these days I'll take you to a place that serves something other than hamburgers and fries."

Kylie smiled as he led the way to their table. To save time they had decided to grab a quick lunch at Burger King. "I don't mind," she said, as butterflies began floating around in her stomach. Did he realize he'd just insinuated that he would be taking her out again?

"It's not too crowded," he said, pulling the chair out for her.

"No, I guess the lunch crowd has come and gone."

"Which is fine with me. Before I go order, I think I need to do this." He pulled off his tie and stuffed it into the pocket of his jacket. Then he reached for the top of his shirt and worked a couple of buttons through the holes. "I'm a little too overdressed for this place."

Kylie watched as he walked off toward the counter, thinking that an overdressed Chance was the last thing on her mind. Thoughts of an undressed Chance seemed to be cemented into her brain. In a suit it he looked handsome, professional and suave. And she would bet that even in a pair of jeans and a shirt he would look rugged and sexy. She didn't want to think about how he would look without any clothes on at all. But she had, several times, day and night, and that wasn't good.

It didn't take long for him to return and they began digging into their food. It was only when they were halfway through their meal that Chance spoke. He leaned in close, smiled and said, "I was wondering about something."

"What?"

"Since we've assigned ourselves the task of monitoring our kids' behavior, to make sure they stay out of trouble, whom should we assign to do the same thing for us?"

Chapter 4

That was a good question, Kylie thought as she held Chance's gaze from across the table. Who would make sure the two of them stayed out of trouble?

The smile on Chance's lips matched the one in his eyes. Still, she knew that, like her, Chance realized this was a serious discussion. A part of her wished she could forget that he was Marcus's father and that they'd met because of their children. But she couldn't forget, even while her attention focused on nothing but the shape of his mouth. It taunted her to lean in and cop a taste.

She drew in a deep breath, trying to regain control, and got a sniff of his cologne. The manly scent of him was unnerving, totally sexy.

"Don't look at me like that, Kylie."

She blinked and saw more than a bare hint of challenge in his eyes. She didn't have to wonder just how she'd been looking at him. The throb between her legs told the whole story and then some. It was a deep ache and it was all she could do from asking him to relieve her of her pain.

She was astounded with her lack of strength where Chance was concerned and wished she could ignore how he made her feel, dismiss the longings he stirred inside of her. But at the moment she couldn't. At least not while her heart was beating a mile a minute and the heat was taking her body to an intolerable degree.

Regardless, she knew she had to fight temptation and take control. She wasn't a lustful teenager. She was a grown woman of thirty-one. A woman with a teenage daughter she should be concerned about. Tiffany was important. Tiffany was the only thing that mattered.

With all the strength she could muster, she broke eye contact and busied herself with pulling napkins out of the holder. "I don't want this, Chance," she said, knowing he knew full well what she meant.

He nodded. "To be honest with you, I don't want it, either, Kylie. So tell me how we can stop it."

She shrugged. It wasn't as if she had any answers. She was definitely lurking in uncharted territory. The only thing she knew was that around him she had the tendency to feel things she'd never felt before. No man had ever made her breathless, excited and hot. When it came to the opposite sex, she felt just as inexperienced as her daughter. Oh, sure, she'd engaged in sex before, and at the time she'd thought it was pretty good, once she'd gotten beyond the pain. But Sam had been just as young and inexperienced as she had been, and she figured what she'd always thought of as satisfaction was nothing more than an appeasement of her curiosity and the elation of finally reaching womanhood at the hands of someone she thought she loved.

But she wanted more than that for Tiffany. More than teenage lust eroding what could be a wonderful experience with the man she married. That was the reason she was sitting here, a little past one, with the sexiest man alive. It wasn't about them. It was about their children. They needed to realize that and get back on track.

"I think the first thing we should do is to remember the reason we're here in the first place.

You have a business to run and so do I, but our kids take top priority. Nothing else. My wants and needs have always come second to my daughter's and things will continue to be that way, Chance."

She paused briefly before she continued. "It's going to take the two of us working together to keep things from going crazy between Tiffany and Marcus. Shifting our concentration from them to us will not only make us lose focus, but will have us making some of the same mistakes they'd be making."

"So, you're suggesting that we pretend we don't have urges and that we aren't attracted to each other? You think it will be that easy?" he asked.

The frustration in his tone matched her own feelings. "No, it won't be easy, Chance. To be quite honest with you, it will probably be the hardest thing I've had to do in fifteen years."

She thought about the men in her past who had shown interest in her and how she'd sent them away without a moment's hesitation. There had been that new guy at work who tried hitting on her several times; then there was that guy who worked at the post office who had enjoyed flirting with her. Not to mention that handsome man at the grocery store who gave her that "I want to get to know you" smile.

But none of them had piqued her interest like Chance had. None of them had offered any temptation. Chance was too incredibly sexy for his own good. Even worse, he was a pretty nice guy.

"We have to keep our heads," she said. "Or the kids will take advantage without us realizing it." Kylie hoped—prayed—that he wouldn't give her any hassles. They needed to be in accord. They needed to be a team with one focus.

He leaned over the table, closer to her. "I know you're right but…"

She lifted an arched brow. "But what?"

"At this very moment, the only thing I want is to kiss you."

His blatant honesty, as well as the heat of his gaze, burned her. She could actually feel the flame. His softly uttered words only intensified the throbbing between her legs, and made fiery sensations rip through her stomach. It wouldn't take much for her to lean in to him and mesh her lips with his, satisfy at least one craving they evidently both had. And without any control, her body began doing just that, leaning closer…

They jumped apart at the sound of a car backfiring. Kylie's eyes widened and her cheeks tinted with embarrassment. They were sitting in the middle of Burger King thinking of sharing a kiss, for heaven's sake!

"Are you ready to go?" Chance asked.

Kylie drew in a deep breath. Yes, she was ready. The sooner she got back to the shop the better. There, she could regain her sensibilities, take back control of her mind. No doubt Chance had more experience dealing with this sort of thing than she did. Regardless, she knew she couldn't depend on him to keep things in perspective. An affair with Chance was the last thing she wanted. No matter what, she had to remember that.

"Thanks for lunch, Chance," Kylie said to him as he backed out of Burger King's parking lot.

"You're welcome. I enjoyed it."

For the next few minutes they shared pleasant conversation in which he told her about his parents retiring to Florida and about his three brothers and three female cousins. It wasn't hard to tell that the Steele family was close.

"So how is your flower business?"

She appreciated him asking. It was a good idea to stick to general conversation. "So far business is good. Before moving here I did my research, made sure adding another florist wasn't over-crowding the market."

"You have a good location since it's an area ripe for development."

"Yes, and I owe it all to Lena. She put her real estate skills to work and gave me a call one day. It was just what I was looking for, exactly what I needed. I grow a lot of my own plants in the greenhouse out back. Those I don't grow I get from a pretty good supplier."

She paused briefly as he glanced over at her. He hadn't put back on his jacket or tie, which made her wonder if he planned to go back to the office or just chill the rest of the day. She scolded herself when she realized what Chance did was really none of her business.

"If you don't mind, I need to make a stop. It won't take but a couple of minutes. I promise to get you back to your shop before two."

"All right."

She blinked seconds later when he pulled up to a car wash. She thought his SUV looked pretty clean. It was definitely in better condition than her car.

"I have those pesky bugs on my fender," Chance said, as he eased his truck into the bay.

The automatic equipment began moving around the truck, blasting water over it and hiding them from the outside world in a cocoon-like waterfall. The insides of the truck suddenly got dark, intimate, warm.

She didn't want to but she couldn't help but

glance over at Chance. Seeing the seductive look in his eyes, she knew this was no coincidence. Coming here had been deliberate on his part.

"This is the first time I've done this. I've never brought a woman with me to get my truck washed," he said in a husky voice. "But I want to kiss you, Kylie."

Kylie swallowed at the passion she heard in his voice. She hated admitting it but she wanted to kiss him as well. But still...

"Chance, I thought we decided that—"

"Please." His tone vibrated with a need that touched her when she knew it shouldn't. "Ten minutes is all I ask."

Kylie blinked. *Ten minutes? A car wash took that long?* As if reading the question in her eyes, he said, "I'm getting a heavy-duty wash."

"Oh." Still, she'd never been kissed for ten minutes.

"Come here, Kylie. Please."

The knot in her throat thickened. She knew he wanted her to slide over to him, and heaven help her but she wanted it, too. Without stopping to question the wisdom of her actions, she unsnapped her seat belt and scooted toward him. When she got close enough he pushed back the seat and pulled her into his lap. His arms automatically closed around her shoulders as he held her in a warm embrace.

"Thank you," he said huskily, before sweeping his tongue across her lips and taking her mouth, hungrily, thoroughly. The first touch of his mouth on hers had her automatically parting her lips. And now with the insertion of his tongue, he brought out a responsive need in her so deep, she began to intimately stroke his tongue with hers.

She had never been kissed this way, had never known that such a way was possible. But it was clear as glass that Chance had a special, skillful technique. His tongue was stroking the top of her mouth, sliding over her teeth, entwining his tongue with hers, sucking relentlessly on it.

Her breasts, pressing against his chest, felt full, sensitive and tight. Instinctively, she wrapped her arms around his neck as they greedily consumed each other. She tasted every inch of his mouth while pressed against him, feeling the way his body had hardened beneath her bottom.

The kiss went on and on as his mouth continued to take hers, skillfully, thoroughly, tantalizing every bone in her body and making her conscious of just what a master he was at igniting sensations.

And they were ignited—by sensations she had

never felt before. She was experiencing the emotions of a woman and not a sixteen-year-old girl. In reality, this was her first taste of passion and Chance was delivering it in grand style.

There was a need hammering deep within her that she didn't understand, but evidently Chance did, since he seemed to sense just what she wanted, just what she needed, even if she wasn't certain. The only thing she was sure about was that he had taken their kiss to a level she hadn't known possible.

The sound of a car door slamming made her remember where they were and what they were doing. The honking of a horn indicated that someone was behind them waiting for their vehicle to move. Still, Chance took his time easing his mouth from hers. She could barely think. She could barely breathe. And she could barely break the connection of the dark eyes locked with hers.

"I think the truck is clean enough now, don't you?" he asked throatily against her moist lips with a sound that sent sensuous chills down her body.

Kylie didn't trust herself to speak at the moment. When he released her, she slid out of his lap and back across the seat. She'd read about women being kissed senseless but never in her wildest dreams had she thought such a thing was possible. Boy, had she been wrong.

She snapped her seat belt back in place as she felt the truck move forward. When they were back in the sunlight, a dose of reality struck. They'd been in the midst of making out in his truck like teenagers. She inhaled deeply, wondering how she could have let things get so out of hand.

"It was inevitable, Kylie."

She glanced over at him. Just because what he said was true didn't mean she liked hearing it.

"Please don't have any regrets," he said softly.

How could she have regrets when she had been a willing participant, just as much into the kiss as he had been? However, she did intend to have her say. "We need to have more control, Chance. How can we expect our kids to have control if we don't?"

He pulled the truck to the side and parked it, and then glanced over at her. "They're kids, but we're adults, Kylie. Our wants and needs are more defined than theirs. And a lot more profound."

"Sounds like a double standard to me."

"It's not. That kiss we shared has nothing to do with our kids. That was strictly personal, between me and you."

She stared at him, hoping he understood what

she was about to say. "I don't have any regrets about the kiss but it can't happen again, Chance."

A slow smile played across his lips. "That's easier said than done, Kylie. I tasted your response. You're a very passionate woman, moreso than you even know. You've denied yourself pleasure for a long time and now that your body has savored just a sampling, it's going to want more."

She didn't like what he was insinuating. Okay, so she had been a little greedy back there, but still, she had her morals.

"And your principles have nothing to do with it," he said as if he'd read her mind. "So don't even think it. It's about needs that are old and primitive as mankind. I have them and you have them, too."

She frowned. "And I'm supposed to jump into bed with any man just to appease him?"

"No. Only with me."

He evidently saw the startled look in her face, because he then added, "But I'm willing to wait until you're ready."

Kylie inhaled and decided it would be a waste of her time to tell him that no matter how much she had enjoyed their kiss, when it came to an affair, she would never be ready. Especially not with him.

* * *

Another night and Chance couldn't sleep a wink. But at least tonight he wasn't being kept awake wondering how it would be to kiss Kylie since he'd gotten a real down-to-earth experience earlier that day.

And it had been better than he'd imagined.

The moments their lips had connected he had felt a slow sizzle all the way to his toes. The more he'd kissed her, the more she had wiggled closer for a better connection, and while his truck was getting the wash it really hadn't needed, he was inside with her locked in his arms, and getting hotter by the second.

She had felt like she belonged in his arms and the firm breasts that had been pressed against his chest had felt like they were meant to touch him that way. More than once he had been tempted to ease his hand under her blouse and cup her breasts, massage them, lift her blouse and lower his head and actually taste them.

The only reason he had finally lifted his mouth from hers had been to breathe in some air. He had heard the car behind them blowing the horn but he would have stayed right there and ignored the sound if he hadn't needed to breathe. What he'd told her was true. She was one responsive woman but he hadn't meant it as a bad thing. He was beginning to realize that everything about Kylie Hagan was all good.

He glanced over at the clock. It was a few minutes past eleven. He wondered if she was still awake. He reached for the phone, deciding there was only one way to find out.

Trying to get to sleep that night was torture for Kylie. The vivid memory of their kiss in Chance's truck, her sitting in his lap while his tongue stroked her mouth into sweet heaven, kept her wide awake.

She remembered the feel of her breasts, their fullness, their sensitivity, and how at one point she had wanted his lips to bestow the same magic on them that he was giving her mouth. Then there was the feel of his body growing hard beneath her bottom. She would have given anything to feel that same erection cradled into the *V* of her thighs.

Feeling frustrated in the worst possible way, she was about to get out of bed when her telephone rang. She reached over and picked it up. "Hello."

"I just wanted to hear your voice one more time tonight."

Kylie breathed deeply at the seductiveness of

Chance's tone. She had wanted to hear his voice again, too, but hadn't had the nerve to call him. He was definitely bolder than she.

"Kylie?"

She swallowed hard before saying, "I'm here."

"Yes, but I wish you were here."

She shook her head. "That's not a good idea."

"Your opinion and not mine."

"We all have opinions."

"Yes, and we all have the capability of getting a good night's sleep. At least some of us do."

She lifted her eyebrows. Was he having trouble sleeping as well? "Try counting sheep."

"I tried that and it didn't work. Any more suggestions?"

She pulled herself up in bed and relaxed against the huge pillow. "We could talk."

"About what?"

"Anything you want to talk about—except what happened this afternoon."

There was a pause, and then he said, "Okay, fair enough. I'll let you choose the topic."

"All right. Tell me about Marcus. Whenever I ask Tiffany about him the only words she can fix her mouth to say are, 'Oh, he's simply wonderful.'"

Chance chuckled. "Hey, I'm the kid's father. Do

you expect me to admit to any of his flaws? If she thinks he's wonderful, then who am I to disagree?"

"Be serious, Chance."

Evidently there was something he sensed in her voice that let him know she needed to know about Marcus before actually meeting him on Sunday.

"On a scale of one to ten with ten being exceptional, I'll give Marcus a nine. He isn't perfect but for the past sixteen years he has been a son any father would be proud to claim. He's smart, and he's also sensitive, something he inherited from his mother. Cyndi was a warm, loving and sensitive person."

The undisguised love she heard in his voice let her know that he had cared for his wife very much. "How old was Marcus when his mother died?"

"He was nine and he took her death hard. Thankfully, he had my parents, Cyndi's parents and my brothers and cousins. Still, there were times when I worried about him. I made Cyndi a promise the day before she died that I would do everything within my power to make sure that Marcus had all the opportunities that we either didn't have or didn't take advantage of, especially when it came to college."

She nodded. No wonder he was so intense about his son staying focused to get into a good university.

"Marcus knew of his mother's dreams for him and after she died it was as if he was trying to honor her memory by doing everything that she'd wanted. He was always at the top of his class, and I never had to remind him to do homework. He tried so hard to please me because I think in his mind, pleasing me meant pleasing his mom as well."

"And then here comes Miss Tiffany...."

Chance chuckled again and in her mind she could actually see a smile lighting up his eyes. "Ahh, yes, here comes Miss Tiffany. But before Tiffany came football. I hadn't wanted him to play. I had played in school and I knew how grueling practice could be. I wasn't sure Marcus could handle it and still keep his grades up. I think that was the first time the two of us butted heads."

After a pause he said, "Luckily he had his uncles on his side. It took my brothers to make me see that I was being unrealistic and that it wasn't all about making good grades. Marcus had a few more years in high school to go, and kids these days need to be well-rounded and I was keeping him from being that."

"So he started playing football?"

"Yes, and the girls started calling...and calling and calling. My phone was a regular hotline. But I think they annoyed him more than captivated his interest. At least until Tiffany."

"Tiffany used to call your house all the time?" Kylie asked, somewhat surprised.

"No, and that's what's so strange. I can't recall her ever calling. That's why I was taken aback when I found that note and was stumped further when Marcus told me, in no uncertain terms, just how he felt about her. It was as if she appeared one day out of the clear blue sky."

Kylie nodded. It was as if Marcus had appeared out of the clear blue sky as well. He'd definitely been one well-kept secret.

"Now it's your turn."

"My turn?" Kylie echoed.

"Yes, to tell me all about Tiffany so I can be prepared."

Kylie's lips tilted into a smile. "I don't think anyone can ever get fully prepared for Tiffany. She's smart, funny and extremely outgoing. An extrovert if you've ever seen one. I think that's why she's having trouble making friends at school since we moved here. I don't think the kids know how to take her. They see her genuinely exuberant nature as being insincere and phony."

Kylie's smile then widened. "There is, however, something that I do think you should know."

"What?"

"I told Tiffany that as Marcus's father you would want what was best for him."

"And?"

And she feels certain that you're going to like her when the two of you meet because she is definitely the best."

Chance laughed. "Sounds like a person with a lot of confidence."

"A little too much at times. It comes from her dad's side of the family."

"Hey, there's nothing wrong with having an over-abundance of confidence."

"Remember you said that when you meet her on Sunday."

There was a hint of amusement in Chance's voice when he said, "I will. And by the way, is there anything you need for me to bring?"

"Yes, a lot of prayer just in case Tiffany and Marcus don't want to go along with our plans for them."

"Hello."

"Marcus, are you awake?"

Marcus clutched the phone as he buried his head back underneath his pillow. "Tiffany, it's Saturday morning. Nobody gets up before eight on Saturdays."

"I do. Some of us have chores to do and the earlier they get done the better. I only called this time of the morning because you said your dad always plays basketball every Saturday morning with his brothers, and you told me to call if I had anything to report."

Marcus removed the pillow. She had gotten his attention. "And you have something to report?"

"Yes. Your dad called here last night. And it was late."

Marcus lifted a curious eyebrow. "How do you know?"

"Your phone number showed up on our caller ID this morning and it showed the time as close to midnight. That means our parents are talking after-hours. That's a good sign."

"But what if he just called to get directions to your house or something?"

"At midnight? Think positive, Marcus."

"Okay. But we should be able to tell if anything is going on when we see them together tomorrow, right?"

"I hope so, Marcus."

"Yeah, I hope so, too, considering how much of a pain in the butt I've been to my dad over the past week."

Chapter 5

By the time Chance and Marcus arrived at Kylie's home on Sunday evening, Chance was chomping at the bit to see her again.

The moment they pulled into her driveway, he saw her standing in the backyard in front of a barbecue grill. Kylie looked up the moment she heard his truck and their gazes connected. His gut clenched when an irrepressible smile lit her face.

"Wow! Tiffany was right. Her mom is a knockout," Marcus said with such profound amazement that Chance sharply turned his head to look at his son.

Marcus's gaze was glued to Kylie, so Chance let himself stare at her, too, letting his eyes roam over her features. Kylie was a beautiful woman, and that was the main reason he—a man known to have good self-control—had been in such a bad way since meeting her. She was wearing a sundress and the turquoise color flattered her.

"Isn't she pretty, Dad?"

Chance swallowed. In his book she was more than pretty, or beautiful or even gorgeous. There wasn't a word he had to define just what she was, although the word *perfection* came pretty close. And not for the first time he wondered how she'd succeeded in keeping men at bay all these years.

"Dad?"

He knew his son was waiting on his response but he dared not look at Marcus for fear of him recognizing the lust in his eyes. "Yes, she's pretty."

Moments later, Marcus asked, "Aren't we going to get out?"

Feeling a lot more confident that he had regained a semblance of control, Chance glanced over at Marcus. "You sound rather anxious."

Marcus chuckled. "I am. I want you to meet Tiffany. She's really something else."

Chance nodded as he opened the door to the

truck, thinking that, evidently, it ran in the family, because he thought Kylie was something else as well.

As Kylie watched Chance get out of the truck, she could no more stop the flash of desire and excitement that raced through her body than she could have denied her next breath. And to make matters worse, Chance's eyes were glued to her and she knew he was remembering their kiss as much as she was.

She had thought about it a dozen times since it had happened. Her response to him had surprised her, overwhelmed her, until she'd come to grips with the fact that Chance Steele wasn't your typical man.

Today he was wearing a pair of jeans and a crisp white shirt, and it was the first time she'd seen him dressed in anything other than a suit. He looked the epitome of masculinity, fine and sexy.

She forced her gaze from him to the young man walking by his side. So this was Marcus, the potential root of her troubles. He favored Chance and was almost as tall. He had the look of youth, but like his father, Marcus's features were sharp and well-defined. And she was glad to see that he eschewed the popular baggy pants and was dressed neatly in a pair of shorts and a shirt. It wasn't lost on her that he was checking her out with as much curiosity as she was him.

"I hope we aren't too early," Chance said, breaking into Kylie's thoughts when they reached her.

They *were* early; a good thirty minutes to be exact, but she didn't have any complaints. "No, Mr. Steele, you're right on time," she said, addressing him formally. They had decided not to let the kids know they had been in constant communication with each other. They didn't want to run the risk of Marcus and Tiffany thinking they were gaming and plotting behind their backs, even if they were.

"Tiffany is inside getting dressed and I was setting up the grill. I hope hamburgers and hot dogs sound okay."

Chance chuckled. "You aren't trying to pay me back with the hamburgers, are you?"

"Pay you back for what?" Marcus asked.

Both Chance and Kylie glanced at him. "Nothing," Chance said quickly, clearing his throat. She knew he hadn't meant to let that slip.

"You must be Marcus," she said and then gave him her full attention and offered him her hand.

His grin was unrepentant as he took it. "Yes,

ma'am. And you've got to be Tiffany's mom. You're pretty just like her."

Kylie smiled. This kid was a real charmer and before the evening was over she intended to see if his charm was the real thing or not. "Thanks."

"Do you need our help with anything, Ms. Hagan?" Chance asked, glancing around at her big backyard.

Kylie looked up at him and smiled. "I think it would be fitting if you called me Kylie, that is if you don't mind me calling you Chance."

He smiled. "No, I don't mind at all."

"In that case, Chance, there is this one little thing I might need help with. Tiffany thought it would be a good idea to put up the volleyball net in case anyone was interested in playing after dinner. If I can get you and Marcus to set it up, that would be wonderful."

"Consider it done. Just tell us where it is and where you want it to go."

"It's over there and I think that would be a good spot," she said, turning to point to an area of her yard.

"I think so, too. That should be fun. I haven't played volleyball in years."

"Should I be worried about that, Dad? I don't think we have anything for sore, aching muscles at home," Marcus said, grinning.

Chance's mouth curved into a smile as he glanced over at his son. "I might be a lot older than you, Marcus Pharis Steele, but I think I can still manage to hit a ball or two over a net."

That's not all he's capable of doing, Kylie thought, shifting her gaze from Chance to Marcus. No matter what disagreements they might have had since Tiffany had appeared on the scene, it was rather obvious that Chance and his son had a close relationship.

"You're going to have to prove that big-time, Dad."

"Hey, kid, you're on," Chance countered and then turned his attention to Kylie. "What do you think?"

"I think that this I got to see," she told him, laughing.

"You'll more than see it. I want your participation as well. The young against what this pup considers as 'the old'. I think we need to show our children just what we're made of. How about it, Kylie?"

She grinned. "I'm game if you are."

"Mr. Steele?"

Chance cast a quick glance over his shoulder, blinked and did a double take. He turned around and blinked again, shaking his head in disbelief. He looked into the face of what had to be a younger version of Kylie. Her daughter looked so much like her it was uncanny. He watched as her mouth curved into the same type of smile Kylie wore.

He automatically smiled back. "Yes, and you must be Tiffany," he said, taking the hand she offered. "Marcus has told me a lot about you."

"And it was all good, right?"

Chance chuckled, remembering what Kylie had said about her daughter's high confidence level. "Yes, it was all good."

She glanced around. "And where is Marcus?"

"I sent him to the store to pick up some more sodas."

"Oh. Mom told me to tell you that she'll be back outside in a minute. She's finishing up the potato salad and thought I should come out and keep you company."

He smiled. "That would be nice since I'd like to get to know you. So what are your plans for the future?" he asked as he leaned against the stone post holding up the covered patio. Kylie had assigned him the task of cooking the hamburgers and hot dogs, something he had convinced her he was pretty good at.

Tiffany laughed. "You don't have to worry about me and Marcus rushing off doing anything stupid when we become of age, like getting married or something."

Chance grimaced. God, he hoped not. "That's good to hear. What about the two of you making plans to cut school again?"

She grinned. "Okay, I admit that wasn't a smart idea, but like I told Mom, our last two periods of the day are boring."

Chance folded his arms across his chest and regarded her directly. "And I'm sure your mom told you that it doesn't matter how boring the classes are, you and Marcus belong in school."

Tiffany's expressive eyes filled with remorse. "Yes, sir, and Marcus and I talked about it. We didn't intend to get you and my mom upset with us, but Mom thinks I'm too young to start dating and you—"

When it seemed that she had encountered some difficulty in finishing what she was about to say, Chance lifted an eyebrow. "I'm what?"

She leaned in closer and squinted her eyes against the smoke coming from the grill. "Don't take this personally, Mr. Steele, and Marcus says you're a nice dad and everything, but at times you can be too overbearing where his education is concerned."

Chance couldn't help but laugh. He was being told that he was overbearing by a fifteen-year-old girl! She might have inherited her high confidence level from her father but her directness had definitely come from her mother. "Marcus thinks I'm overbearing, does he?"

"Yes, and you don't have to be, you know. Marcus is one of the smartest guys I know. In fact, the way we became such good friends is because the teacher had him help me on a class assignment that I was having problems with. He wants to go to the best college one day, just like you want him to. You're just going to have to trust him to do the right thing. And he will because he wants those things for himself as well as for you."

Chance's smile widened. Tiffany's expressive eyes had gone from being filled with remorse to being filled with sincerity and he liked that. He also liked what she was saying, and had to admit that his curiosity was piqued about something. "And where will all this leave you, Tiffany?"

"Me?"

"Yes, you. Where will that leave you when Marcus goes off to college two years from now?" Assuming your relationship lasts that long, he wanted to add.

Tiffany shrugged. "When he leaves I'll have another year of school to complete and then I'll be leaving for college myself. I doubt it will be to the same college Marcus will be attending since my grades aren't nearly as good as his, but it won't matter. Marcus and I have decided that the best thing for us to do is to make sure we both get a good college education. Then we will return home afterward and be together."

Chance's eyebrows drew together in surprise. The last time he and Marcus had talked, his son had threatened to hang around Charlotte and go to a local college. He released a satisfied sigh. He was certainly glad to hear this recent turn of events and was about to tell her so when they heard his truck pulling into the driveway, which meant Marcus had returned.

"Mr. Steele, Marcus and I can finish cooking if you want to go into the house and keep my mom company. I'm sure she's bored making the potato salad."

Thoughts of being inside the house alone with Kylie had his mind reeling. "You think so?"

"Yes."

He rubbed his chin thoughtfully. "Have you told your mom what you and Marcus have decided about your futures?"

"No, not yet."

"Do you mind if I do?"

"No, I don't mind. It's not like me and Marcus won't be girlfriend and boyfriend until he leaves for college, because we will. But we won't let anything interfere with him going away to a good university, I can assure you of that. We want what's best for our future." Then with a smile on her face she said, "I'll go help Marcus with the sodas."

Chance watched her walk away, thinking he really liked Tiffany Hagan.

"So what do you think?" Tiffany whispered to Marcus while helping him unload the soda from the truck.

Marcus grinned. "I think my dad likes your mom. In fact I have a feeling that they may have seen each other another time in addition to that day he visited her flower shop."

"What makes you think that?"

"Because they're too friendly with each other to have met only that one time. And then there was this private joke they shared."

"What private joke?"

"It had something to do with hamburgers."

"Hamburgers?" Tiffany raised a confused brow. "So you think he likes her?"

"He definitely notices that she's a woman, which

is more attention than he's given other ladies, including those at church who are always vying for his and my uncle Morgan's and my uncle Donovan's attention. They know it's a lost cause with Uncle Bas since he's already engaged."

After placing the soda cans in the cooler, Marcus continued. "When we pulled up today and I saw your mom for the first time, I commented on how pretty she was and he agreed with me. And he kept staring at her with this funny look on his face. He's been smiling a lot since he got here. I don't recall ever seeing my dad smile this much."

Marcus then gave Tiffany a questioning glance. "You do think we're doing the right thing, don't you? Making our parents think something is going on between us so we can get them interested in each other?"

Tiffany nodded her head. "Yes, I think we're doing the right thing. I have to admit that at first I was doing it just to get Mom off my back because I thought she needed a life, but today she was actually humming. She was humming because she's in a good mood, and I think the reason she's in a good mood is because of you and your dad's visit. Seeing her that way made me realize just how lonely my mom probably has been. All she's ever had is me. Like I told you, I don't ever recall her dating anyone. In a few years I'll be leaving for college and she'll be all alone if she doesn't meet someone and get serious about him."

Marcus nodded. "Yeah, Dad will be all alone when I leave for college, too, in two years. He has his parents and his brothers and cousins but it won't be the same. He needs to get involved with a nice lady like your mom. I really like her."

When they reached the backyard, Marcus glanced around. "Speaking of our parents, where are they?"

Tiffany's face glowed with excitement when she said, "My mom is inside making the potato salad, and I suggested to your dad that he go inside and keep her company, and that you and I were capable of doing the cooking."

Marcus smiled down at her. "It seems our plan just might be working."

Tiffany tipped her head back and looked up at him, returning his smile. "Yes, it certainly appears that way. Now it's going to be up to us to make sure they get to spend more and more time together."

Chance strode into Kylie's house, rounded the corner that led from the utility room to the kitchen and stopped dead in his tracks. For the first time in his life, he forgot how to breathe.

Kylie was standing on a stool trying to get something out of a top cabinet. Stretching upward, the sundress she was wearing had raised, showing off a pair of luscious hips and those legs of hers that he admired so much.

His conscience gave him a hard kick. He shouldn't be standing in the middle of her kitchen ogling her this way. The truth of the matter was that he couldn't help it. The tantalizing sight of her had captured his attention and wouldn't let go. Pure, unadulterated hunger filled his gaze, keeping him focused primarily on her. She had a gorgeous body and, with the fantasies playing around in his head, he could just imagine his hands all over it, followed by his mouth.

He inhaled deeply when he felt his body getting hotter by the second. The need to escape back outside suddenly overwhelmed him. He had to get out of there, right now, this very instant, before he went up in flames or—even worse—before he did something outside of his control like cross the room, snatch her off that stool and take her into his arms and kiss her senseless.

Kylie wasn't certain if she'd heard a sound behind her or if her own body had alerted her to the fact that

Chance was near. Whichever it was, she turned around so fast that she almost slipped off the step stool and had to fight to regain her balance.

Within an instant she was gathered into strong arms, avoiding a possible fall.

"You okay?"

The soft husky words from Chance's lips that fanned against her temple raised her temperature ten degrees. "Yes, I'm okay. You startled me. I hadn't heard you come in."

Instead of offering her any kind of explanation, he simply nodded as he held her body in his strong arms. For the next couple of seconds her mind questioned the sanity of them standing in her kitchen that way. What if the kids walked in?

She panicked at that possibility. "I'm okay, Chance. You can put me down now," she said, although she knew her voice lacked conviction.

"Are you sure you're okay?" he asked, his tone deep and rich, and his gaze remaining steadily on hers.

No, Kylie thought. She wasn't sure. Desire, the likes of which she'd never encountered before, raced through her, igniting her awareness, her attraction and her fire. Her eyes locked with his and at that instant she felt safe and protected in his arms, even with the feel of his body growing hard beneath her, which reminded her of the kiss they had shared Friday at the car wash.

With her teeth she caught the edge of her bottom lip, thinking she was just where she had dreamed of being last night—in his arms. Would it be so terrible if she stayed there just a little longer?

"Where are the kids?" she asked softly, tilting her head back and not breaking eye contact.

"Outside, cooking the rest of the meat."

"That should take at least five minutes."

"I'm counting on at least ten," he said.

She felt him sliding her down his body, lowering her feet to the floor. But he kept his hand at her waist, not intending for her to go anywhere out of touching distance. When she was standing, her legs automatically parted slightly to gain her balance; ironically it was just enough room for him to pull her close and place his thigh between them. She felt him again, the hardness of his erection that was resting between her legs.

"Why didn't you let me know that you had come inside?" she asked as intense heat shot up her core.

An apologetic smile touched his lips. "I couldn't have spoken even if I had wanted to, Kylie. Seeing you on that stool like that had me barely breathing.

Has anyone ever told you that you've got one hell of a nice figure?"

She tried not to be touched by the thought that he liked the way her body looked. "Yes, but it never really mattered."

"Oh."

"Until now."

He bent toward her. "You're sure?"

"Positive."

He intended to be certain of that. Moving his hand to the swell of her hips, he gently pulled her closer as he leaned down and slanted his mouth over hers. She tasted sweeter than he remembered and he was helpless to do anything but deepen the kiss. He knew the exact moment she placed her arms around his neck, bringing their bodies closer into a locked embrace.

What he was sharing with her was a degree of passion he hadn't shared with any woman in over seven years, and he was desperate for anything and everything she was offering. He suddenly felt it, a primitive need to bind her to him in the most elemental way. But he also knew he wanted more from her than just her body. He wanted her mind and soul as well.

The sound of their kids' laughter came through the closed window and they parted quickly, but he didn't release her. Resting his forehead against hers, he breathed in deeply, seeing the passionate look in her eyes and knowing it mirrored his own.

He motioned his head toward the back door. "You don't think they're outside burning our dinner, do you?" he asked, making an attempt at gaining control.

"I hope not," she replied, trying to breathe again normally.

"I came inside to keep you company. Tiffany suggested it."

"Did she?"

"Yes. Is that a bad thing?"

"Only if it meant doing so would give her more time alone with Marcus."

Chance gave her an incredibly sexy smile. "I didn't think of that. But I guess there's only so much they can do outside in the open."

Kylie smiled. "Thank heavens for that."

"And she happened to mention something to me that she said she hadn't told you about yet."

"What?" she asked, her voice barely above a whisper, hoping whatever it was would not make her fall dead in a faint. She had asked, and Tiffany, although upset with her for asking, had assured her that she was still a virgin.

Evidently Chance heard the panic in her voice and an easy smile touched his lips. "Relax, Kylie, that isn't it. Far from it."

"Thank goodness for that."

"I personally don't think they've taken their relationship to that level, which is a good thing. In fact I'm a little more confused than before by what she said, although it pleases me."

"Dammit, Chance, don't keep me hanging," Kylie said in a near desperate voice. "What did Tiffany tell you?"

"Our kids have decided that although they intend to remain girlfriend and boyfriend, they also intend to further their education by going off to college, after which they'll return here and then decide their future."

Kylie blinked. "Are you sure that's what she said?"

"I'm positive."

She shook her head. "It doesn't make sense. Earlier this week she was ranting and raving about how madly in love they were and nothing and no one would ever break them apart."

"I heard the same thing from Marcus. I guess they sat down and talked about it and in the end decided to take our advice. They were getting too serious way too fast."

"Whatever made them decide to slow things down, I'm extremely grateful for it. Do you think we still need to lay out the rules we came up with?"

Chance nodded. "They may think this way now but it might be a different story tomorrow. Besides, either way, there's plenty of trouble they can get into before Marcus actually leaves for school in two years."

And it was the kind of trouble Kylie was definitely familiar with. She agreed with Chance. It wouldn't hurt to let the kids know exactly where she and Chance stood and how they planned on handling the situation of them being a couple.

"Ready to go outside?" he asked.

"Just about. I just need to find that lid for the bowl of potato salad. That's what I was looking for when you came in."

"Then let me look for it."

Kylie watched as he crossed the room and, not needing a stool, reached up and opened the cabinet. He pulled out several lids. "Will one of these work?"

"Yes."

He placed them on the counter then crossed the room to her. He reached out and caressed his finger against her cheek. "Thanks for the kiss, Kylie. I needed it more than you will ever know."

He really didn't have to thank her. She'd needed it just as much as he had, although she wished she hadn't. "I think we need to get back outside now."

As much as Chance wanted to stay inside with her, a part of him knew she was right. "All right. Is there anything else you need for me to do before I go?"

A smile touched her lips. "No, but it might be a good idea for you to wipe your mouth. You're wearing the same shade lipstick I'm wearing."

"Now that the both of you are well fed, there's something Chance and I would like to discuss with you."

Both Marcus and Tiffany looked up from eating their ice cream. Marcus's smile faltered somewhat and Tiffany rolled her eyes heavenward. "I knew this day was going too good to last," she said. "What do you want to talk with us about, Mom?"

"Your relationship."

"What about it, Ms. Hagan?" Marcus asked her in a respectful tone.

Kylie glanced over at Chance, who nodded for her to continue. "Chance and I talked about the best way to approach the situation, especially since Tiffany isn't old enough to date yet."

"But I should be old enough, Mom. The other girls at my school began going out with boys when they were thirteen."

Kylie frowned. "I'm not going to discuss what the other girls are doing, Tiffany. You're my concern. And for me it's not a particular age but a maturity level. I personally don't think you're ready to begin dating."

"If you had your way I would never date!"

"That's not true. You're the one who has to prove to me that you're ready. But Chance and I do understand you and Marcus would like to spend some time together, so we came up with what we feel is a workable solution."

"And what solution is that?" Marcus asked when Tiffany refused to do so.

It was Chance who responded. "You and Tiffany can date only if the dates are chaperoned."

Tiffany glanced over at Marcus before looking back at their parents. "You mean that you'll be coming with us to the movies? Bowling? On picnics?"

"Yes," Kylie answered. "So what do you think?" She braced herself for her daughter's tirade.

"I think it's a wonderful idea," Tiffany said, smiling.

Kylie blinked. "You do?"

"Yes. Since Marcus and I will be getting married after college, I think it would be good that all four of us get to know each other." She smiled at Marcus. "Don't you agree, Marcus?"

He smiled back at Tiffany. "Right, and in the process we can prove to our parents just how responsible we are."

Kylie glanced over at Chance knowing he was just as confused as she was. Tiffany and Marcus were beaming. If anything, Kylie and Chance had thought their suggestion would be met with some pretty strong opposition.

"Well, if everyone agrees with our plan then that's great," he said.

"So how soon can we go someplace?" Tiffany asked excitedly.

"Where would you like to go?" Chance asked.

"Umm, I've never been camping and Marcus said you take him all the time."

Kylie rolled her eyes. "Tiffany, we're not talking about a family outing. We're talking about a date."

"I don't have a problem with Tiffany coming along the next time Marcus and I go camping," Chance said. "Of course that means that you'll have to come too, Kylie."

"Yes, Mom. You've never been camping before, either."

"Yes, but that doesn't mean we can just invite ourselves on a camping trip, Tiffany."

"But Mr. Steele invited us."

"Yes, but only after you—"

"It's okay, Kylie, honest," Chance cut in to say. "Marcus and I would love for you and Tiffany to go camping with us. My family owns a cabin in the mountains so we're really not talking about roughing it too much. The cabin has two bedrooms, so you and Tiffany can take one and Marcus and I can take the other."

"I'm not sure that's a good idea," Kylie said as her gaze moved from one person to the next. "When Chance and I thought of supervised activities we didn't mean anything that involved staying any place overnight."

"Yes, but it would be fun and different, Mom, and you and I have never done anything fun and different."

Kylie leaned back in her chair. She thought the two of them had done several things that were fun and different. How about that train ride from New York to California a few years ago? And then there was that vacation to Disney World for Tiffany's twelfth birthday. Had it really been three years ago? Okay, so they hadn't actually done a lot of time to do fun and different things together on a regular basis. But she really hadn't had the time since she'd been busy going to school and trying to move up the corporate ladder to provide for her and Tiffany.

"Please, Mom, just this once. Mr. Steele did say it would be okay."

Kylie glanced over at Chance. "Are you sure you don't mind?"

He smiled. "No, I don't mind. In fact I think it's a wonderful idea."

Chance's statement should have had a calming effect on her but it didn't. She was no longer concerned for Tiffany, but for herself. She didn't want to think about a weekend spent in a mountain cabin with Chance in such close quarters. With all the heat they could generate, the kids might think something was going on between them when it really wasn't.

"Well, Mom?"

The enthusiasm she heard in Tiffany's voice almost made her say yes, but a part of her held back. This was something she needed to really think about.

Instead of answering Tiffany, she looked over at Chance. "Let me think about it some more and I'll give you my answer within a week."

Chapter 6

With a sigh of resignation, Chance walked into his office Monday morning and met his brothers' inquisitive gazes. He knew why they were there. Marcus had mentioned to them that they'd been invited to Kylie's for dinner and no doubt they wanted to know how things went. But he wouldn't make it easy for them. He would pretend that he hadn't a clue why they graced his office with their presence.

"Good morning. Is there any reason the three of you have taken over my office?" he asked, placing his briefcase down on his desk.

After a few moments, when no one replied, he exhaled a long sigh and said, "I don't recall us having a meeting this morning. I know I have a meeting with Bas later today, but what's up with you guys? Is any-thing wrong?"

Not surprisingly, it was Bas who stepped forward and said, "How about cutting the bull, Chance. You know why we're here. We want to know how things went yesterday."

Chance looked at him. "Was there a particular way they were supposed to go?"

"You tell us," Morgan said, frowning. "You were the one who was all bent out of shape last week when you found that note. Can we assume you blew things out of proportion and Tiffany Hagan isn't the threat to our nephew's future that you assumed she was?"

Chance leaned back in his chair. A part of him wanted to tell his brothers that Tiffany was no longer a threat but her mother definitely was. But there was no way he could do that and have a moment's peace from their inquisition. "No, Tiffany's not a threat and although I'm not going to say I overreacted, I will say that I think Kylie and I have everything under control."

Donovan quirked an eyebrow. "Kylie?"

"Yes, Kylie Hagan. Tiffany's mother."

Donovan smiled. "Oh, yeah, the one who's such a good-looker."

A dark scowl suddenly appeared on Chance's face and he leaned forward. "And how do you know that Kylie is good-looking?"

Donovan was taken back by the bite in his brother's tone. "You told us, don't you remember? In fact your exact words were, 'If the daughter looks anything like the mother then I'm in trouble.'"

"Oh." Too late, Chance recalled having said that. He leaned back in his chair again, ignoring the curious glances his brothers were now giving him.

"You know what, Chance?"

Chance glanced over at Morgan and frowned. "What?"

A smile curved Morgan Steele's lips. "I hate to tell you this, but I have a feeling that you've gotten yourself into some trouble."

"So there you have it, Chance," Bas was saying after handing him the written report. "I'm glad to say that considering everything, we're doing well. Although some of our competitors have gotten bruised by the severe trading conditions of the past few years, we've been successful because we're a company that sets the pace and doesn't just follow the trend. Still, whether we like it or not, sooner or later we're going to have to give some thought to the possibility of outsourcing in order to stay competitive. I don't like it any more than you, but that's the way things are going now and we need to continue to adapt to change, even change we don't particularly like."

Chance tossed the report on his desk. Bas was right. He didn't like the thought of outsourcing as a means to stay ahead of the game. With the new importance being placed on countries like India and China, for the past year he'd seen huge restructuring taking place in a number of manufacturing and production companies.

As the corporation's problem solver and troubleshooter, Bas kept them in the know. He was an expert at tackling the company's complex problems. So far the Steele Corporation was not unionized because, during the twenty-five years of its existence, the employees had always been pleased with the fair treatment they'd received. Their salaries were more than competitive, and the Steele Corporation had a reputation of never having laid off an employee, even during some of the company's rough times.

However, according to Bas, there was talk in the production area that the Steele Corporation would be outsourcing to a foreign country.

"I'm still not ready to go that route, Bas. Our employees are loyal and we owe them for all the hard work they do. Our people are the reason this company is successful, not the products we produce and deliver. What we're going to have to do is to continue to focus on developing our employees and executing those manufacturing strategies that integrate people, processes and technologies to assure us tangible results. Until that stops happening, I refuse to entertain the thought of outsourcing to another country."

Bas smiled. "I fully agree with you. So what do we do about those rumors that we're headed that way the first of the year?"

"Before I leave for Dallas next week, how about setting up a meeting between me and the production department heads? I want to make sure they're delivering the same message to our employees. There's evidently a communication breakdown somewhere. And make sure you include Vanessa. She will be back in the office then," Chance said of his cousin Vanessa Steele who headed the PR Department and was presently vacationing in Europe.

"All right. Consider it done."

Chance studied his brother as Bas placed the items back into his briefcase. Bas was a hard worker—too dedicated at times since he lived, ate and breathed the Steele Corporation. That would make one wonder when he had time for a social life, which he evidently had since he was engaged to be married. "Seems to me that you need to chill more than I do, Bas."

Bas glanced up and his lips curved into a lethal half smile. "I beg to differ, Chance. You're the one who's tackling woman troubles. I'm not."

"It's hard to believe Cassandra is that under-standing."

Bas shrugged. "Frankly, she's not but she knows how far to take her complaints."

A frown pulled at Chance's lips. Not for the first time he wondered what had possessed his brother to become engaged to Cassandra Tisdale, a staunch member of Charlotte's elite social group. Cassandra and Bas were as different as day and night. The woman was so incredibly self-absorbed, it boggled Chance's mind that Bas had even given her the time of day, let alone become engaged to her. She had a tendency to think she was the most important thing that existed in this universe. And while she was shining and polished, it was known that Bas was more than a little rough around the edges and had a few tarnished spots on his reputation from a few years back. But Cassandra was determined to do something nobody had ever been able to do—make Sebastian Steele sparkle.

Chance and his two brothers wondered how in the hell she planned to accomplish such a feat. If nothing else, they would give her an A for trying. They knew, even if she didn't, that it would be a wasted effort. The woman who would eventually capture Bas's heart would be the one who accepted him as he was, and not try to make him into something that he wasn't.

"Dinner is at six tonight, if anyone is interested," Chance decided to say, since his brothers had a tendency to drop by for a meal unannounced.

Bas chuckled. "I'll pass the word on to Morgan and Donovan."

"What about you?"

"I'm invited to dinner at the Tisdales'. My guess is that Cassandra's mother will try to get me to finally commit to a June wedding."

Chance nodded. That was eight months away. "Will you?"

"There's no reason for me not to, I suppose. Being

engaged for almost six months is long enough, don't you think? See you later."

When the door closed behind Bas, Chance stood and walked over to the window and looked out. Deciding to rid Bas and his issues from his mind, he turned his thoughts to his own problem.

Kylie Hagan.

He couldn't help wondering whether she'd made a decision about the camping trip yet. Several times that day he'd been tempted to call her but had changed his mind.

He felt excited at the prospect of having her at the cabin for an entire weekend, even with the knowledge that their kids would be around to keep them company. It would be hard to keep his attraction to her at bay, but he would.

He figured the reason she was hesitating was because the thought of them spending the night under the same roof bothered her. She was well aware that the kids would have to go to sleep eventually, and when they did, it would be parents' time.

She was fighting the chemistry between them. He knew that just as he knew it was a fight she wouldn't win. But he would let her try, up to a certain point. He'd give her until the end of the week and if he didn't hear from her by then, he would take some necessary action.

* * *

"So, have you decided whether or not you and Tiffy are going camping with Chance Steele and his son?"

Kylie glanced up from the meal she and Lena were sharing during their weekly lunch date at a popular restaurant in town. "Who told you about that?" she asked.

Lena smiled. "Who else? My goddaughter, of course. She's all excited at the thought of going camping."

Kylie rolled her eyes. "I'm beginning to wonder if it's the camping trip that has her excited or the thought of being around Marcus an entire weekend. If it's the latter then she might as well get unexcited because if I do decide to go, I'll have my eyes on her and Marcus the entire time. Any time they spend together will definitely be supervised."

Lena couldn't help the small smile that tugged at her lips. "So you think she has an ulterior motive for wanting to go?"

"Hey, remember I was young and in love once, and when you are their age, you look for every opportunity to be together, whether you're under your parents' watchful eyes or not."

"Yes, that could very well be, but at some point you're going to have to start trusting her, Kylie. You can't continue to judge Tiffy by the way you behaved with Sam. The more you do, the more she's going to resent it."

There was anguish in Kylie's eyes and a wee hint of guilt. "It's so hard being a parent these days, Lena. You want the best for your kids and you go on the premise that experience is the best teacher, but then you're faced with the question of how you can be there to protect them without suffocating them."

Lena nodded, clearly understanding. "I think for you it's more difficult because Tiffy is all you have. Over the years she has become your life. Have you given thought to becoming involved in other things?"

"Other things like what? I have a florist shop to run, Lena. It's not like I don't have anything else to do with my time."

"Yes, but only when Tiffy is at school. Other than that you're a full-time mother who really doesn't have a life other than her child."

Kylie knew where this conversation was leading since they had been down this road several times. It was the one topic she and Lena didn't agree on. Lena felt it was a crying shame that she didn't have a man in her life and hadn't had one since high school.

Her thoughts shifted to Chance Steele and how much she had enjoyed his company on Sunday. It had felt strange sharing her time with anyone other than Tiffany, but she had to admit it had felt good, too. Too good. After they'd eaten they'd played a game of volleyball, the young against what Marcus and Tiffany had considered as "the old."

Kylie had been surprised at how much energy Chance had. The kids had been surprised, too, and she and Chance had won the game, showing Tiffany and Marcus that age was nothing but a number. Afterward, they had eaten ice cream and the cake she had baked.

As much as she had enjoyed Chance's company, she knew it was out of the question for something to develop between them. There was no way she would start depending on him or any other man for her happiness. She had done so once and refused to go that route again.

"I don't want a man in my life, Lena, at least not now," she decided to say. "Maybe when Tiffany leaves for college I'll feel differently and I'll get involved with someone, but I'm not interested now." She then turned her attention back to her meal.

"Okay," Lena said, placing her glass of iced tea aside. "Tell me about Chance Steele."

Kylie looked up again, giving her friend an uncomfortable stare. "What do you want me to tell you about Chance that you don't already know?"

"Well, Tiffy couldn't stop singing his praises when I picked her up from school yesterday. He definitely made a positive impression on her. She thought he was cool and fun to be around."

Kylie smiled. "She's right. He was a lot of fun."

She quickly resumed eating her meal, afraid that Lena might see all the lust that filled her eyes. The last thing she wanted was to tell Lena that Chance was the cause of her surging hormones lately. Which was exactly why she didn't think going on a camping trip with him, Marcus and Tiffany was a good idea. The longings he stirred within her could be relentless at times, and it took all the will power she could muster to hold on to her sanity. Her needy libido and her out-of-control hormones confined in a cabin for the weekend with Chance Steele were way too much to ignore. Especially when she'd have to stay focused on Marcus and Tiffany.

"Chance is not a bad catch you know, Kylie. He's good-looking, wealthy, intelligent and generous to a fault."

Kylie glanced up. "Umm, sounds like someone you should be interested in, then."

A sad smile tugged at Lena's lips. "You know the story of my life. Because of Mom's failing health, the two of us are a package deal and not too many men want that. At least none I've met so far. The moment I mention that I'm my mother's caretaker, they conveniently drop out of the picture. However, I do believe Chance would be different, but he and I never connected that way. I can only see him as a friend and nothing more."

Unfortunately, Kylie could see Chance as a lot more than a friend but she blatantly refused to go there. But right now, at that moment, her main concern was not the issue of her and Chance. It was Lena. She silently searched her mind for something to say that would ease the raw pain she'd heard in her best friend's words.

Propping her chin in her hand, she gave Lena a serious smile. "There's a man out there for you, Lena, who will be more than happy to take you and whatever and whoever comes along with you. I've always known that if I got interested in someone, that person would have to love Tiffany as much as he loved me. For some men it's easy to accept a package deal. For others it's not. And those who can't are the ones that women like us do better leaving alone."

Lena reached across the table and took her hand. "And I believe that there's a man out there for you, too, and believe it or not, he can be depended on. I know Sam and your dad let you down but you can't continue to judge all men by their actions, Kylie. Every young girl needs a good male role model in her life. Because of Dad's death, I missed having that, and you're cheating Tiffy of having that as well. I think as a single mom you've done an admirable job in raising her. But don't you think at some point she needs to see you in a loving relationship with a man?"

Kylie looked Lena squarely in the eye. Conversations like this tended to expose emotions that she would rather keep under wraps because along with the emotions came the memories of the hurt and pain that Sam and her father had caused.

"Even if I did, Lena, that man can't be Chance Steele. For heaven's sake, he's the father of the boy that my daughter thinks she's madly in love with."

Lena placed her elbows on the table and laced her fingers together. "And what does that have to do with anything? More specifically, what does it have to do with you and Chance?"

"I don't want to confuse her, nor do I want to send out a negative picture about anything."

Lena shook her head. "Your daughter and my goddaughter is a lot smarter and mature than you think, Kylie. Kids these days know the score. They aren't as naive as we want to think they are. If something is going on between you and Chance, she'll be able to pick up on it, and personally, I doubt if she'll see anything wrong with it."

"She might not see anything wrong with it but I will. How am I going to lecture her about the difference between love and lust when I'm having problems knowing the difference between the two myself?"

Lena smiled. "So you are attracted to Chance." It was a statement and not a question.

"Yes, more than I want to be," she said, deciding to finally be completely honest with her best friend. "Around him I feel things that I've never felt before, Lena. We've kissed. Twice. And I'm not talking about a little kiss, either. The man takes kissing to a level I've never experienced before. All he has to do is get close enough to breathe on my mouth and my lips automatically open. Isn't that pathetic? Now can you understand why I'm hesitating about going on that camping trip?"

"Yes and no."

At Kylie's confused expression, Lena explained,

"Yes, I can see why you're hesitant about going, and no, I don't agree with your assessment of the situation. So what if you have the hots for Chance? You're both adults and should be able to do whatever you want to do. Your attraction to him shouldn't have any bearing on what's going on between Tiffany and Marcus and how you're handling their situation. I know you and no matter what you do, you will always set a good example in front of Tiffany. However, what you and Chance do in private is your business. But then, like I said earlier, I think it's important for Tiffy to see you in a loving relationship with a man, and I can't think of a better person for that man to be than Chance Steele."

"There are bound to be complications, Lena."

"Only those of your own making, Kylie. Take it from someone who knows. Good men are hard to find, so if you meet one who's interested, you better grab him, hold on tight and not let go."

Later that night Kylie got into bed, wrestling with the knowledge that the main reason she didn't want to go on that camping trip was because of her growing feelings for Chance. She had to finally admit those growing feelings to herself after having lunch with Lena.

Their discussion had made her realize two things. She found Chance attractive and sexy, and thought he had a body that was all that and a bag of chips. But there was more to him than that. He'd already proven that he was dependable, unlike Sam and her father. When Chance and his girlfriend had been faced with a teen pregnancy, instead of leaving her in a fix like Sam had done to her, Chance had done the noble, honorable and responsible thing. He'd made whatever changes the situation called for to make a home for his wife and child. She could tell by his relationship with Marcus that he was a good father and from what she read in the business section of the *Charlotte Observer*, he was also a highly respected businessman. And she wanted to believe if he had shown up at her shop that day to tell her that their kids were involved in an unplanned pregnancy versus a plot to cut school, he would be angry, true enough, but nothing would make him turn his back on his only child, as her father and mother had done to her.

She sighed. One of the problems she was having trouble coming to terms with was the knowledge that their relationship—if they could call it that— had developed because of their kids. She doubted they would have met any other way. There was a strong possibility that if they'd been in the same room together at any given function, he wouldn't have given her a second look. So in her mind their meeting was a twist of fate rather than by their own choosing.

She jerked her head off the pillow at the sound of the phone ringing. The last time she had gotten a call this late it had been Chance. Sensations raced through her at that possibility and she quickly reached over and picked up the phone. "Hello."

"Sorry to call so late," Lena was saying. "But I forgot to mention today that the American Cancer Society is sponsoring their annual ball and I'm on the committee. The price of the tickets is high but it's all for a worthy cause, of course. Would you like one?"

Before Kylie could answer, Lena quickly inserted, "In fact you can get two if you like and bring a date."

"I'll take one ticket, Lena," Kylie said softly, hoping Lena didn't pick up the disappointment in her voice. A part of her had hoped the caller was Chance. She hadn't seen or talked to him since Sunday, which was three days ago.

"Sure you don't want two?"

Kylie rolled her eyes. "No, I only want *one* ticket,

Lena. I won't have a date that night. Will that be a problem? I either come alone or not at all."

"No, that won't be a problem but I was hoping there was someone you could ask. Someone like Chance, perhaps?"

Kylie sighed. She knew where this conversation was leading and wasn't in the mood. "No. Only one ticket, Lena. Good night." She then hung up the phone.

A few seconds later, before Kylie could reclaim her comfortable position in bed, the phone rang again. She frowned. There were times when Lena was worse than a dog with a bone. She didn't know when to let up.

Snatching the phone, not giving her best friend a chance to say anything, Kylie said, "Look, Lena, forget it. There's no way I'm going to ask Chance to go with me."

There was a brief pause and then…

"And just where is it that you won't ask me to go, Kylie?" Chance Steele asked in a deep, husky voice that bespoke more than mild curiosity.

Kylie's eyes widened and hot color rushed into her face. If she'd been standing she would have melted to the floor in embarrassment. Instead she found solace in burying her face under the pillow.

But even that couldn't drown out the sound of Chance's voice when he said, "Okay, Kylie, tell me. What's going on and why won't you ask me to go wherever it is that you're going?"

She closed her eyes and moaned. Her only saving grace was that she'd heard the teasing in his voice and was glad he had such a good sense of humor, even if it was at her expense.

"Kylie?"

She pulled her head from beneath the pillow. "What?"

"Are you going to tell me voluntarily or do I have to come over and tickle it out of you?"

The thought of Chance actually tickling anything out of her had a stimulating effect on her rather than an amusing one. Yet she couldn't help but smile. "I doubt if you can tickle anything out of me, Chance."

"Don't let me come over there and prove you wrong," he warned in an even huskier tone of voice.

Kylie closed her eyes and in her mind she could envision him lying in bed saying what he'd just said. He would be propped back against the pillow with a sexy smile on his lips and a teasing glint in his dark eyes.

She allowed her mind to go a little further by

envisioning him lying on top of the bedcovers completely naked. Her overactive imagination spread warmth through her as she envisioned her gaze moving down his muscular chest and firm stomach before coming to rest on his exposed groin. He was hard as steel.

She inhaled deeply and wondered what it would be like to touch him there, caress his body all over, bury her face in the curve of his neck, taste his skin and nibble him in a few places to brand him hers. She would let his musky scent fill her nostrils before pressing her mouth to his, getting the deep, tongue-tangling kiss she knew awaited her. She would let her hand reach down to touch him in his most private area, feeling the heat of him, hot, hard and thick. The mere thought of seducing him that way had blood racing recklessly through her veins.

"Kylie?"

She swallowed, trying to bring her thoughts back in check. "Yes?"

"Tell me."

The sensuous tone of his voice was playing havoc on her sensibilities. She leaned back in bed, letting her body cool from the heated thoughts that had flowed through her mind earlier. Her lids lowered and for a long second she didn't say anything, wondering if she should. But she knew he wouldn't let up until she told him.

"Lena mentioned that the American Cancer Society is having their annual ball and she's on the committee," she started off by saying. "So quite naturally she's trying to get rid of as many tickets as she can. I told her I'd get a ticket to support the cause and then she tried talking me into getting two, knowing full well I wouldn't have a date that night."

"And?" he asked when she paused briefly.

That single, softly uttered word stirred an area of her body that it shouldn't have. "And...Lena suggested that I invite you."

"So that's what you meant when you screamed in my ear."

Color rushed into Kylie's face again. "Yes, that's what I meant."

"I see. Don't I have a say in the matter?"

"No. The only reason we met, Chance, is because of the kids," she said, giving voice to her earlier thoughts. "If we had been at any function together you wouldn't have noticed me. I'm not the type of woman you would have been drawn to enough to show any real interest in."

"You think not?"

"Yes."

"What if I said you're wrong?"

"We'll never know, will we?"

When he had no comeback, she said, "Besides, I don't date. I mentioned that to you before."

"Yes, you did mention it. Is that also the reason you won't go camping, because you see that as a date?"

"No, that in itself is a whole other set of problems, Chance. I just think the two of us spending a weekend at a cabin isn't a good idea, even with the kids there. Especially with the kids there."

"Why?"

"I think you know the reason without me having to go into any great detail. For some reason, we're like magnets—we attract."

"And you see that as a bad thing?"

"Yes. Our focus should be on our kids. What would Marcus think if he thought you were attracted to me?"

Chance chuckled. "He would probably think the same thing I did when I finally got to meet Tiffany. That he has great taste. She's a nice girl and so is her mother."

Kylie couldn't help but smile, pleased with his compliment, but still… "Can't you see the problems it will cause if our kids think something is going on between us?"

"No."

"Chance," she said, moaning his name in frustration.

"Kylie. We've had this conversation before and my feelings on the matter haven't changed. We're adults and what we do is our business. In fact I think Marcus will find it strange if I'm not attracted to you. He thinks you're beautiful, so quite naturally he'll assume that I'll think you're beautiful, too. And I do. I also think you're someone I'd like to get to know better. He would assume as much as well. But you're right. The camping trip will be about Marcus and Tiffany and not about us. Our time will come later."

She wondered what he meant by that.

"Will it make you feel better if I promise to be on my best behavior when we go camping?"

Kylie shrugged. How could she explain to him that his behavior really had nothing to do with it? It was her own behavior she was concerned about. He didn't have to do anything in particular for her to get turned on. Her dilemma was the fact that just seeing him did that.

"If you don't go, you know what might happen, don't you?"

Chance's question recaptured her attention. "No, what?"

"The kids are going to feel that they can't depend on us to keep our end of the bargain. We did tell them that we would agree for them to take part in supervised activities."

"But we never said anything about overnight activities, Chance."

"Neither did we clarify they had to be only daytime activities. They won't understand what the big deal is since we will be there as chaperones. They will only see it as a cop-out on our part. I don't think it's fair to cancel out a weekend of fun for them just because we can't keep our hormones in check for forty-eight hours. It makes us sound pretty damn selfish, don't you think?"

Kylie sighed deeply. It hadn't before, but since he'd put it that way, yes, it did make them—her in particular—sound selfish. Tiffany had never gotten the chance to go camping. Kylie had been too overprotective to even let her go with the Girl Scouts that time when she was ten. And now all her daughter wanted was to experience her first camping trip and her selfish mother, who couldn't keep her overactive hormones in line, was standing in her way.

"Okay, you've convinced me. I'll go."

"Great! The kids will be happy."

She laughed. "Yes, I'm sure they will be."

"I'll make the arrangements for next weekend. Will that work?"

"Yes, that will work."

"And. Kylie…?"

"Yes?"

"The kids aren't the only ones who'll be happy. I'm going to be happy as well. Good night."

Before she could say anything, he hung up the phone.

Chapter 7

A few days later Kylie was praying that at some point her life would resume a sense of normalcy. Since she'd told Tiffany of her decision to go camping, her daughter had been nothing but a bundle of mass excitement. So much, in fact, that Kylie had to wonder whether being with Marcus was the primary reason for her daughter's happiness or the camping trip itself.

With teenage exuberance, Tiffany had gone on and on about all the things she planned to do, like swimming in the lake, fishing in that same lake, having a picnic by that lake and taking oodles and oodles of pictures of that lake. And she intended to do a lot of bird watching and had even checked out a library book on the various species. Of course that meant she would need a pair of binoculars, which her godmother had been quick to buy for her.

Kylie hadn't talked to Chance anymore until he'd called early Saturday morning saying he would drop off a list of items she might want to bring along. The cabin's kitchen was well-stocked with cooking utensils, but he thought it would be good if they cooked outside on the grill or a camp stove. He'd gone on to tell her that although the cabin had elec-. tricity, usually he and Marcus enjoyed faking it by using candles and lanterns.

Anticipating his visit, she had been a mass of nerves, and once she opened the door not even the loud wail of a fire truck siren could intrude on her jolting awareness of him. She pulled in a deep breath. And then another. Neither did a thing to stop the pounding of her heart or the barrage of sensations that overwhelmed her.

Standing before her in jogging pants, a T-shirt and a pair of what appeared to have once been expensive tennis shoes, Chance Steele was the epitome of everything hot and spicy. He looked like a man capable of doing anything he pleased, whether it was in the boardroom or in the bedroom. Especially in the bedroom. However, at that very moment she had to concede that there was nothing sophisticated about Chance's appearance. He looked like a man ready for some play time, and his darkly stubbled jaw, which meant he hadn't yet shaved that morning, only added to his sharply male features.

"Here's the camping checklist I told you about," he said, breaking into her heated thoughts.

She took the paper he handed her. "Thanks."

"The only things you'll need to bring for you and Tiffany are the items listed under the first-aid section."

She nodded and quickly scanned the list, okay with everything she saw on it until she noted the snake bite kit. She lifted her gaze back to his. The eyes that met hers were dark, sexy and full of sexual interest he wasn't trying to hide, which made her thankful for two things: that she was a woman and that she was decently dressed. "Snake bite kit?"

A smile touched his eyes. "Yes, just as an added precaution. But I have one if you have trouble finding it. It's a rather popular item this time of the year."

An uninvited shiver ran through her. That wasn't exactly what she wanted to hear. She cleared her throat. "Would you like to come in? Tiffany and I were just sitting down to breakfast. You're welcome to join us."

"No, thanks. I'm on my way to the gym. It's tradition that my brothers and I play basketball every Saturday morning. It helps get rid of any competitive frustrations we might have before the start of a new week."

She lifted a brow. "Competitive frustrations? Does that happen often?"

"I guess with four adult males it can't help but happen occasionally, given the closeness of our ages and our competitive natures. Then of course there's Donovan, who often forgets that I'm the oldest and he's the youngest."

It wasn't the first time she felt that an extreme closeness existed between the Steele brothers. It was there in his tone whenever he spoke of them. "Well, enjoy your game."

"I will. And just so you'll know, I'm catching a flight out first thing Monday morning to Dallas. I'll be there until Thursday. Marcus will be spending time with my brothers until I return."

"All right, thanks for letting me know," she said, missing him already, although she didn't want to feel that way. "Have a safe trip."

By the way he was staring at her, she knew without a doubt that if Tiffany hadn't been home he would have come inside and kissed her goodbye. That knowledge caused an ache in certain parts of her body. Their connected gazes were holding just a little too long. She knew it and was fully aware that he knew it as well.

"I'll call you," he finally whispered huskily.

Kylie nodded. A promise made and one she knew he intended to keep. "All right."

She wrapped her arms around her waist, hugging herself so she wouldn't be tempted to reach out and hug him.

He took a step back and looked deeply into her eyes one last time before turning back to his truck.

During the next four days Kylie spent her free time shopping for the items on the list Chance had given her. After that was done, Tiffany had convinced her that they needed to spruce up their wardrobes, with a collection of new outfits suitable for camping.

Kylie enjoyed this carefree, happy-go-lucky side of her daughter. It had been a long time since she'd seen it and she couldn't help but count her blessings now.

She and Tiffany returned home from one of their shopping trips rather late on Wednesday night and were in her bedroom unwrapping their numerous packages.

"Mom, can I ask you something?"

"Sure, honey, you can ask my anything."

"Why don't you have a boyfriend?"

Kylie's hand went still on the new blouse that she was about to place on the hanger. You can ask me anything but that, she wanted to say but decided it was a good question. If only she could give her daughter what she felt was a good answer. She decided to go for the truth...but only after she found out why Tiffany wanted to know.

"Why do you ask?"

"Because I think you're so pretty and all the other girls at school whose moms are single always talk about their mothers' boyfriends. In fact Trisha Nobles's mom is getting married next month."

Good for Trisha Nobles's mom, Kylie wanted to say. But she knew the only reason Tiffany had asked the question was because the answer was important to her.

"I've been too busy to have a boyfriend," she said honestly. "Running the shop takes up a lot of my time."

"But even before we moved here and you worked for that marketing firm you never went out on a date or anything."

Kylie lifted an eyebrow. "And that bothered you?"

"I really never thought about it until recently."

Kylie sat on the bed next to her daughter. "And why recently?"

"Because now I know how it feels to care for some-one and I think it's sad that you never cared for anyone before. It doesn't seem right."

Kylie pulled her daughter into her arms and was mildly surprised when she came willingly. "Oh, honey, but it's okay. Some things aren't just automatic. Another reason I never went out was because I'm a very selective person."

"Nitpicky?"

Kylie laughed. "Yeah, nitpicky. Only a certain type of man appeals to me."

Tiffany pulled back and glanced up at her. "Really? And what kind is that, Mom?"

Kylie immediately thought of Chance and forced him from her mind. "First and foremost he has to be willing to be a good father to you. Then he has to treat us both good, look good, be health-conscious, fun to be around, be someone I can always depend on even during my darkest hour, and someone who loves me unconditionally."

"Unconditionally?"

"Yes. Someone who would love me no matter

what and who would take me as I am—the good, the bad and the ugly."

Tiffany smiled. "You know that's funny."

"What is, honey?"

"Marcus said he recently asked his dad why he never remarried. And it seems that he's nitpicky, too."

"Really?"

"Yes. And he gave almost the same exact answers as you did." Tiffany chuckled. "Boy, adults sure are strange."

"Strange in what way?"

Tiffany gave her mother a beaming smile. "If all of you are looking for the same thing in a person, then why is it so hard to find someone?"

Before Kylie could answer her daughter's question—not that she thought she had an answer anyway—the phone rang. Tiffany quickly picked it up. "Hello?"

Kylie watched her daughter's dark eyebrows lift curiously. "I'm fine, and yes, sir, she's here. Just a moment please."

Her daughter then stared at her with bright, penetrating eyes and whispered, "It's for you and it's Mr. Steele. He's probably calling to make sure that you got everything on that list for the camping trip this weekend."

Kylie took the phone her daughter handed her. "Yes, I'm sure that's why he's calling," she said, trying to keep her voice neutral but feeling she'd failed miserably. She hoped Tiffany hadn't picked up on any-thing.

"That's really nice of him to call us all the way from Texas, isn't it?"

"Yes, it is."

"Well, it's late and I have school tomorrow so I'm going to bed. Thanks for taking me shopping, Mom. Good night."

"You're welcome and good night, sweetheart."

With quiet gravity Kylie watched Tiffany leave the room, closing the door behind her. It was only then that she turned her attention back to the phone and the man waiting on the line to talk to her.

"Hello?"

"Sorry about that, Kylie. I assumed Tiffany would be in bed by now."

"Usually she is but that's okay. I took her shopping after school and we just got back a little over an hour ago."

Chance chuckled. "Must have been some shopping trip."

Kylie smiled. "Trust me, it was." She didn't want to sound too excited but she was glad to hear his voice. "How are things going?"

"Busy. This is one of those annual meetings where the CEOs of various corporations get together, leave egos at the door and work on something we all need to improve within our companies."

"And what's that?"

"Employee relations. But I didn't call to talk about that. I wanted to see how you and Tiffany were doing."

"We're fine." Actually there was something concerning her. Maybe Chance could shed some light on it. "I know Tiffany talks to Marcus every day, but I'm a little concerned about something."

"What?"

"Although I told him on Sunday that it would be okay if he wanted to visit with Tiffany for a few hours after school on occasion, he hasn't done so."

"Umm, even with football practice I'm surprised he hasn't jumped at the chance at least once. Does Tiffany seem bothered by it?" Chance asked.

"No, and I know for a fact that they aren't mad at each other." Kylie sighed. Maybe things were different with teenagers today. She and Sam had practically tried living out of each other's pockets. It had gotten so bad that he had become a regular fixture around her parents' house although they had wished otherwise.

"Maybe I'm assuming too much here, Chance, but I thought with them being so 'madly in love' that once I gave the go-ahead for supervised visits that Marcus would become a constant visitor."

"That's strange, because I know that I would."

"You would what?"

"Become a constant visitor if you ever gave me the go-ahead."

Chance's voice was hardly more than a whisper but she heard the underlying meaning loud and clear. Kylie's breath hung in her throat for a brief second and then she took a deep, calming inhale, which was followed by a series of flutters in her stomach.

"Kylie?"

"Yes?" She was glad to say anything, even that one single word, to assure her that her vocal cords were still working and they hadn't drowned in all those sensations overtaking her.

"May I ask a favor of you?" Chance asked.

"Sure," she said with a small shrug, certain he wouldn't ask her to do anything indecent or immoral.

"Would you pick me up from the airport tomorrow around lunchtime?"

Surprise flickered in the depths of her dark eyes. "You want me to pick you up?"

"Yes. My car is at the dealership getting serviced while I'm away. I can get one of my brothers to pick me up but I would like for you to...if it won't be any problem."

"No, it won't be a problem. But can I ask you something?"

"Yes."

"Why do you want *me* to do it?"

"You'll find out when I see you."

The sound of his voice held promises she wasn't sure she wanted him to keep. She'd been having a lot of mixed emotions since meeting Chance. A part of her knew that getting involved with him was not a good idea, but then another part of her—the one that lately was constantly reminding her that she was a woman with needs—was egging her on to enjoy what he was offering. At least within reason.

"All right. Would you like to give me your flight information now?" For the next minute or so, she jotted down the information that he gave her.

"Well, I'll let you go now. I'm sure the shopping trip tired you out."

"Yes, it did somewhat. I appreciate you calling."

"I told you I would. I just hope my doing so hasn't raised Tiffany's suspicions. I know how much you don't want the kids to think anything is going on between us."

"No, I don't think your call did. In fact she said she thought it was very considerate of you to call and make sure we were all set for this weekend."

"And are you all set for this weekend, Kylie?"

More than I need to be, she thought, thinking of all the new outfits she had purchased with the hopes that he'd like each and every one of them. "Yes, I found all the items on the list including the snake bite kit."

"Good girl. Now do something tonight when you go to sleep."

"What?"

"Think of me."

Chance settled back in the bed after placing the phone back in the cradle. He hadn't been able to concentrate on the summit all week, because Kylie was on his mind. Hell, for the last couple of nights, he hadn't been able to sleep a wink.

It had been during Horace Doubletree's speech that day when he'd suddenly came to the realization that it was a waste of time trying to fool himself any longer and that things for him had moved past him trying to get to know Kylie better. The truth of the matter was that he knew all he wanted to know. His heart had decided. He had fallen in love with her.

How such a thing was possible he wasn't sure; especially when the woman had been sending out conflicting signals since the day they met. She was attracted to him, although she was determined to fight that attraction every step of the way. Her independence, while a turn-on, had ironically become a major obstacle to the relationship. That meant he needed to probe deeper and somehow break through her defenses. He also needed to take one day at a time and wipe away the fifteen years of hurt and pain she'd endured and prove that with him there would only be happier days. Even without her realizing she'd been doing so, for the past couple of weeks she had been extracting an unusual type of strength from him.

A strength of will.

He'd been fighting an intense longing, a deep-rooted desire for her since that day he'd walked into her florist shop. He could now admit that the first time their eyes had connected his heart had slammed into fifth gear. No wonder lunch at the Racetrack Café had seemed fitting as a place for their first date. Even then he'd known that something special was within his grasp.

After Cyndi died he'd actually thought that he could never love another woman again. And even with the few affairs he'd indulged in over the years, he'd never allowed his emotions to go any deeper than affection or desire. Yet here he had fallen hard for a woman whom he had never actually taken out on a real date, had never slept with and had never really spent more than a few hours with at a given time. His brothers would say such a thing was utterly insane. They would call in the shrink to have his head examined, or they would take him out somewhere and beat some sense into him. But then they would one day realize that some things in life were not meant to be understood, just accepted. Today he had accepted the fact that he had fallen in love.

And he knew he had his work cut out for him.

There was more than gentle pride in every bone in Kylie's body. He knew just from the time he'd spent with her that she could be stubborn, willful and defiant. That was all well and good if she was dealing with any other man than him. But he refused to wait around for her to bolster her courage to take a chance and fall in love again—this time with a man who wouldn't let her down. He still wouldn't rush her into doing anything, but he definitely planned to show her how good things could be between them. He planned to jar her emotions, jump-start her heart and make her stare the truth in the face.

There were chances in life worth taking and he was one "Chance" she should definitely take. In high school he and his brothers had been pegged as guys who were forged of steel. It was time to prove to Kylie that no matter what, he was a man with the endurance to withstand just about anything.

The next day at noon Kylie was at the airport waiting for Chance to arrive. As usual, no matter what day of the week it was, Douglas International Airport was busy. People were scurrying to their connecting flights or to their rendezvous with their loved ones.

When Chance's flight number was announced, she turned and glued her eyes on the gate. Evidently he traveled in first class because it didn't take long for him to exit the jetway. He was dressed in an expensive suit, and his stride was long and confident as he passed through the gate. There appeared to be an aura of power and authority surrounding him. Chance Steele was one dynamic, compelling and forceful man.

He looked so dependable, like the kind of man at whose feet a woman could leave her worries knowing he would take care of them and she wouldn't ever have to carry them on her shoulders again. He also looked like the kind of man who could drive a woman crazy with desire. She could definitely attest to that.

Her breath caught the moment their gazes met and she felt that immediate quiver of anticipation in her middle. He was going to kiss her. Somehow she knew, and heaven help her but she wanted that kiss more than anything.

She watched his long, elegant stride eating the distance separating them. And with each step he made, a delicious heat inched its way through her veins, making her blood hot and leaving her wondering, not for the first time, how this particular man could affect her so. He was the type of man that fantasies were built on, and who made realities even more poignant. And with every step he took toward her, he was making anticipation that much sweeter.

When he was within five feet of her, she saw the undisguised longing on his face. She could actually feel his desperation. There was a lot she didn't understand but at that moment the one thing she did accept was that in less than a minute, now more like a few seconds, she was going to be kissed senseless.

All the while he'd been walking toward Kylie, the one thought that kept churning in Chance's mind was that she was the woman he wanted and needed in his life.

She was the woman he loved.

Other than his mother, he had never kissed a woman at an airport, but that thought was pushed to the back of his mind when he pulled Kylie into his arms and captured her lips with his. And as their lips engaged in one hell of a lockdown, he wished she could feel all the emotions flowing through him at that very moment.

Knowing he had to get a grip before the kiss really turned raw and primitive, he reluctantly pulled back, but kept his arms around her waist, refusing to let her go anywhere. "Now that was worth coming back to," he whispered softly.

Kylie struggled for breath and then noted they had become the center of attention. "We've caused a scene."

He smiled. "Yes, but some scenes are worth causing."

She looked up at him. "Is this what you had in mind when you asked me to pick you up last night?"

He reached out and caressed her cheek. "Not entirely, but it's definitely a start. Come on, let's get my luggage so we can get the hell out of here."

Chapter 8

Kylie couldn't remember the last time she had a problem with keeping her eyes on the road while driving. But Chance's presence in her car was interfering with her concentration and wreaking havoc on her senses.

After claiming his luggage, he had taken her hand as they walked out of the terminal to her parked car. Once he had placed his bags in her trunk, his arms had clamped around her waist, pulled her to him and he'd sunk his mouth down on hers in another kiss. The moment their lips connected, heat had exploded through her and the heavy bulge of his erection pressed to her middle had caused her entire body to ache.

"We've got to stop doing this," she'd said the moment he had released her mouth.

"Why?" he had whispered hotly against her moist lips.

"Because it won't lead anywhere. It's a dead end."

His gaze had pinned her with a measured look. "And what if I told you that I see things differently?"

"Then my response is that you need a new pair of eyes."

"I have very good vision, Kylie." He'd then strolled to the passenger side of her car and got inside.

Bringing her thoughts back to the present, she took another quick glance over at him. He was sprawled in the seat next to her. His muscular body fit nicely into her Altima, although his broad shoulders took up a lot of space. His legs were long and his seat was pushed as far back as it could go to accommodate his height. His head lay back against the headrest and his eyes were closed.

Evidently the trip had tired him out, but not enough to stop him from engaging in a little mouth exercise with her a couple of times. She had begun thinking of their kisses as TST—taste, stroke and tangle—because each time they kissed he tried a new technique on her mouth that centered around those three basic elements.

"You're tired," she decided to say when she came to a traffic light. "Are you sure you want me to take you to the dealership to pick up your truck instead of taking you home? It might be a good idea for you to go to bed."

He opened his eyes, titled his head and let his gaze fasten on hers. "If you were to take me home and I got into bed, would you get in there with me and keep me company?" he asked, his voice low and sexy.

She inhaled deeply. Although he had phrased the question in a roundabout way, technically he had just hinted at the possibility of her sleeping with him. "No. I'd take you home and put you to bed, but I wouldn't get in that bed with you."

He smiled. "Spoilsport."

She chuckled and turned her attention back to the road when the traffic light changed. "I might be at that, but it seems I'm the one destined to keep us out of trouble."

"Some trouble I might like," he murmured in a low voice leaden with exhaustion, before closing his eyes again.

"And what if Marcus had that same attitude?"

"When he gets to my age he's welcome to it, but while he's underage, I decide what he likes and doesn't like. And stop comparing us to our kids, Kylie. Like I told you before, we're adults. They aren't."

"Sorry, I keep forgetting," she said sarcastically.

"It will behoove you to remember. The next time you forget it will cost you."

She lifted an eyebrow. "Cost me what?"

"A kiss. Right then and there. Even if it's in front of those two kids of ours."

She frowned and took a quick glance at him and saw that his eyes were opened and he was staring at her. His expression was serious. "You wouldn't dare."

"I wouldn't count on that if I were you."

And Kylie was smart enough to know not to. She pulled her car into the dealership, parked it and turned to him. "And just what would doing something like that prove?"

"It would prove that our kids wouldn't have a problem with anything developing between us."

"But I'd still have a problem with it. I won't let any man use me to slake his sexual cravings."

In a flash Chance snapped the seatbelt off his body and before she could get out her next breath he loomed over her. Blatant anger was carved in his features. "This isn't about me slaking any sexual cravings, Kylie. But you're so out of practice with men that you wouldn't know that, would you? Well, let me tell you something, not about men in general but about this man in particular," he said pointing to himself. "I won't ever use you just to slake any sexual cravings, so don't try making my wanting you as anything sullied or dirty.

"It's the most natural thing in the world for a man to desire a woman and vice versa. I won't apologize for it. When we do make love, Kylie, it will be a mutual thing. You'll want it as much as I do, so don't kid yourself into believing otherwise. And when it comes to me there's something else you need to keep in mind."

"And what's that?" she asked softly.

"When there's something I want, I won't give up until I get it."

"When we do make love, Kylie, it will be a mutual thing. You'll want it as much as I do, so don't kid yourself into believing otherwise…"

The words Chance had spoken earlier that day woke Kylie up more than once that night. This time she knew she had to deal with them before trying to go back to sleep.

Taking the pillow from the other side of the bed, she wrapped her arms around it and hugged it to her chest, wondering how in the world one man could be so utterly self-confident, so damn arrogant. The nerve of him making such a statement as if it was a foregone conclusion they'd go to bed together. Well, she had news for him, she thought bitterly.

After this camping trip was over she would put rules into place where their relationship was concerned. The only thing between them would be Marcus and Tiffany. As parents they would have some connection in order to keep their offspring on the right path, but that would be as far as things went. It wouldn't bother her in the least if she never saw the infuriating man again.

Turning over on her side, Kylie gazed despondently at the digital clock on the nightstand. It was almost midnight, way too late to be having this sort of conversation with herself. She should be resting peacefully in a sound sleep, but thanks to Chance she was wide awake.

He had upset her so badly that afternoon that it had been a good ten minutes before she'd been able to pull herself together to drive away from that dealership. And twice during dinner Tiffany had asked her if anything was wrong.

And to think she would be spending an entire weekend in Chance's presence. If there were any way she could cancel their plans without disappointing Tiffany she would, but she knew better than anyone how much her daughter looked forward to this trip.

The phone on her nightstand rang and not for the first time she wished that like the phone in the living room this one had caller ID. But somehow she knew it was Chance and reached out and picked it up. "Hello?"

"I need to apologize, Kylie."

It was his deep, rich, husky voice, more than the words he had spoken, that sent a sensuous shiver through her. "Do you?"

"Not for everything—just for getting upset with you. I won't apologize for our kisses. But your words caught me off guard. Never in my wildest dream did I assume you'd think I would want to use you that way."

"Okay, Chance, maybe it was a bad choice of words, but what I was trying to say was that I'm being logical here. I don't see things as you see them, and when it comes to a lot of man-woman stuff, you're right, I'm way out of my league. You aren't. So I have to protect myself."

"You'll never have to protect yourself from me,

Kylie. I'd never hurt you, take advantage of you or use you. I give you my word."

"Thank you."

"But I won't give you my word that I'll stop pursuing you, stop trying to make you want me as much as I want you, stop trying to—"

"Get me in your bed?"

"No, I won't stop trying to get you in my bed, Kylie, because I think that's where you belong. And once I get you there I intend to keep you there for a long time. But it will be for all the right reasons."

"When is an affair good for any reason?"

"When the two individuals agree that it is. You and I have a long way to go, Kylie. We haven't even gone on what I consider a real date. I want that but you don't."

She sighed deeply. "It's not that I don't want it, Chance, it's just that I don't think it's wise, considering the kids."

"So you prefer that we do things behind their backs?"

"No, I prefer that we don't do anything at all. Why is that so hard for you to understand?"

"And just what is it that you're afraid of?"

She was taken aback by his question. "I'm not afraid of anything."

"I think you are."

"Then think whatever you want."

"I will, and right now I think it's time that I show you something, Kylie Hagan."

She didn't like the way that sounded. "Show me what?"

"What this man-woman thing is all about. Like I said earlier today, you've been out of the game for so long you don't know what's acceptable between couples and what's not. Maybe it's time that I start teaching you a few things and—"

"Teach me a few things?" she interrupted shortly.

"Yes, then maybe you'll realize that you're not immune to me as you want to believe. Good night, Kylie."

The phone had already clicked in her ear before Kylie could recover her power of speech.

"Mom, isn't this place simply beautiful?" Tiffany asked in a high-pitched voice that was filled with enthusiasm and wonder.

"Yes, it is," Kylie replied, trying to direct her gaze out of the cabin window and not on Chance and Marcus as they brought in the items out of the truck.

Especially on Chance.

Instinctively, she took one hand and checked

her pulse at her wrist, not surprised to find the strong beat racing beneath her fingertips. Already Chance was having an effect on her. He had shown up at her place wearing a pair of faded jeans and a T-shirt. The moment she'd seen him those wacky hormones of hers began soaring. She wished there was some type of injection she could take to build an immunity against him.

"Mom, you don't sound excited about being here. Are you okay?"

Kylie turned to meet Tiffany's concerned gaze and suddenly felt guilty. The last thing she wanted was her daughter worrying about her needlessly, which would place a damper on all the fun she'd planned for the weekend. "Yes, sweetheart, I'm fine, and it's going to be a wonderful and fantastic weekend. Now let's put this stuff down and go outside to see if Marcus and Chance need our help."

Once they had stepped back outside, Kylie glanced around. The spacious log cabin that sat on the shore of a huge lake blended well with the surroundings. Trees of all kinds provided plenty of shade, as did a sprawling front porch that had several wooden rocking chairs and a rustic porch swing. Kylie had to agree with Tiffany's earlier assessment. The place was beautiful.

"The air is so crisp and clean here. I can't wait until Marcus teaches me how to fish, and Mr. Steele said he would help. Isn't that nice of him?"

"Yes, that is nice of him."

They walked back toward the truck while Tiffany excitedly rambled on about what fun she planned to have and what a nice man Chance was.

"Need us to help carry anything else inside?" Kylie asked Chance and Marcus when they reached them.

"No, Dad and I can handle things, Ms. Hagan," Marcus said, not giving Chance an opportunity to respond. "But remember we don't use electricity, so you and Tiffany might want to unpack and get familiar with the inside of the cabin. Right, Dad?"

Chance smiled. "Right."

Kylie could feel Chance's eyes on her but she refused to look at him. She was beginning to feel ridiculous and out of sorts because a part of her was still upset about yesterday. He, however, was acting like their conversation never took place. To her chagrin, he was in the best of moods.

"So what's for dinner?" Tiffany would have to be the one to ask.

"I thought it would be nice if we grilled something outside on the open fire," Chance said. "Any ideas?"

Kylie saw the opportunity to make peace and seized it. She glanced over at Chance. "Anything but hamburgers," she said softly, as a tentative smile touched her lips.

Chance met her gaze, immediately recognized their private joke and smiled back. "Okay, no hamburgers."

"What about a hot-dog roast?" was Tiffany's suggestion.

"That's a great idea and we have plenty of hotdog sticks to use," Marcus chimed in.

"Okay, all that sounds good," Chance said, as an amused grin eased up the corner of his mouth. "But because I need something a little bit more filling, I'll throw a couple of steaks on the grill, too."

He lifted the last box into his strong arms. "Come on, let's go inside and get this show on the road."

Kylie inhaled a deep breath as she stepped out of the bedroom she and Tiffany were sharing. More than a dozen candles were strategically scattered about and a couple of huge lanterns blazed in the corners of the living room.

She couldn't help but smile, thinking of all the fun they'd had so far. Chance had given both her and Tiffany a quick lesson on camping and had shown them how to assemble a tent in case they ever needed to use one. Roasting hot dogs on the stick had been fun but she'd appreciated Chance's idea of grilling the steaks when Marcus and Tiffany overcooked the weiners.

And then later, before it had gotten dark, Chance had taken her out in a canoe to the other side of the lake. The scenery there had been just as breathtaking with numerous trees, flowering plants and a catfish-filled stream. Kylie smiled and thought that a person could get spoiled by so much of nature's beauty.

"Marcus is out like a light."

Kylie's smile froze when she turned and saw Chance coming out the bedroom that he and Marcus were sharing. She thought he had turned in for the night.

"So is Tiffany." She gave him a curious look and said, "I thought you had gone to bed too."

"Not without first putting out the candles and lanterns. Fire hazards, you know."

She nodded. "I never realized there was so much to know about camping."

"There is but it's an excellent way to get back to nature. My mom agreed up to a point, which is why my parents purchased this place. She didn't mind getting back to nature but wanted all the comforts of home while doing so."

He grinned as he moved around the room to put out the candles and lanterns. "I hate to say this but we had more fun when we left her at home. Dad was too laid back to worry about us turning over in the canoe or eating berries off the bushes without washing them first. And the only reason we have hot and cold running water is because she refused to let us bathe in the lake. Good old Mom always came with a strict set of rules."

Kylie chuckled. "Haven't you figured out yet that's one of the things we're best known for? Your mother sounds like my kind of woman. I would love meeting her one day."

And I intend for you to do just that, Chance thought as he glanced over at her. Mom would be happy to know that her oldest son has found love again.

All the candles were out but one, and the luminescent glow from that one candle seemed to focus on Kylie, making her skin shine with an ethereal radiance. Her hair had been up in a ponytail earlier but now she'd taken it down, and the mass of braids fell in soft waves around her shoulders.

"Well, I guess I'll call it a night and—"

"Will you sit on the porch with me for a while?" he asked.

Kylie looked at him then shook her head. "I don't think that's a good idea."

The corner of his mouth tipped upward into a smile. "Has anyone ever told you that you think too much?"

"Possibly," she said slowly. "But I won't absolutely admit to anything."

Chance chuckled. "I didn't think you would."

"Now who's thinking too much?"

"Oh, that's real rich," Chance said, laughing. "Come on. I think you'll get a kick out of watching the stars." He reached out and offered her his hand and, only after hesitating briefly, she took it.

Chance was right. She was getting a kick out of watching the stars. Sitting here on the porch and rocking in the chair made Kylie realize all the little things she'd hadn't taken time to do before.

"Sure you don't want to come over here and share this swing with me?" Chance asked.

She chuckled as she glanced over at him. "I'm positive."

"But you aren't sitting close to me."

"I'm close enough, Chance."

"I beg to differ."

She shook her head grinning. "Tell me something. Are your brothers like you?"

"No, I'm one of a kind."

"Thank God."

"Hey," he said with affront. "What's that supposed to mean?"

"Let's just say I'm glad after you were born that they broke the mold. I can't imagine another one like you."

"I'll take that as a compliment."

"You would." After a brief moment of silence she said, "Tell me some more about your brothers."

"All right. Like I told you that day at the Racetrack Café, Bas is eighteen months younger than me and he's the troubleshooter for the company."

"He's also the one engaged to be married, right?"

"So we hear."

She stopped rocking and looked over at him, studied his features from the glow of the moon. "Why do I have a feeling that it's one of those 'I'll believe it when I see it' deals?"

"Because it is. Cassandra Tisdale and Bas are as different as day and night."

Kylie raised a brow. "Tisdale? As in Tisdale who owns a number of car dealerships around town? As well as those two restaurants?"

"Yes, the dealerships belong to her father and the restaurants to her uncle. Same family."

"Why do you think Ms. Tisdale and your brother aren't compatible?"

"Because they aren't."

"He evidently thinks they are."

"Remember you're the one who thinks too much. In this case, I don't believe Bas is thinking at all. But I have all the faith in the world that he'll come to his senses before doing something stupid."

Kylie frowned. "You're serious, aren't you?"

"Quite." After a brief moment he said, "But only because I know my brothers, and Bas in particular. All through his life he's been known as the 'not so stainless Steele.'"

"Meaning?"

Chance frowned at the memories. "He was considered the black sheep of the family because he used to get into so much trouble. I guess you can say he went through quite a rebellious stage while growing up. You name it, he probably did it. It was a good thing my father was good friends with Sheriff Blandford since Bas had a penchant for straying to the wrong side of the law. Most of the time it wasn't him but the crowd he hung out with. But you know what they say about guilt by association."

Yes, she knew. "So when did his future change for the better?"

"When he was about twenty. He dropped out of college after deciding he wanted to see the world. He was gone for a year without us knowing where he was most of the time. All we know is that when he returned he had a new outlook on life. He went back to college, graduated with honors and then came to work at the Steele Corporation, starting from the bottom. He was determined to learn everything he could. Now he's a vital asset to the company. I depend on him to keep me in the know and to put out small fires."

"What about the other two?"

"Morgan is Morgan. He has this thing about finding the perfect woman and until he does he won't settle for less. Then there's Donovan, who thinks he was born to have fun. He's serious enough while at work but otherwise there's really never a serious moment with him. My mother predicts he'll probably be the one who lives the longest because he enjoys life too much to get stressed about anything."

"Does that also mean he's having too much fun to settle down and get married?"

"So he claims. He just hasn't met the one woman to tame his game."

"Quite an interesting bunch."

"Yes, they didn't refer to us as 'Forged of Steele' for nothing."

Kylie lifted a brow. " 'Forged of Steele'?"

"Yes. We were known for our endurance. We thought we could outlast anything."

She decided not to ask their endurance in what. "The possibility that Marcus might be a chip off the old block now has me worried. Should I be?"

Chance chuckled. "No, he's a good kid."

"Yes, I noticed and I'm appreciative of that. I was prepared not to like him, you know."

"Yeah, I know, and it was likewise with me and Tiffany. But I like her. You did a good job raising her, Kylie."

"So did you with Marcus."

"Thanks."

Kylie stretched and then stood. "Well, I think I'm going to call it a night."

"Already?"

"It's probably close to two in the morning, Chance, and I still have to take a shower. That checker game you played with the kids lasted quite awhile."

"Only because your daughter didn't know how to play. I've never heard of such a thing. That's un-American."

"Well, I hate to tell you but her mother doesn't know how to play checkers, either."

"Then I guess I'll add that to my list of all the other things I intend to teach you."

"Don't do me any favors."

"Trust me. It will be for my benefit as well as for yours. The more you know and understand, the better off we'll both be."

Kylie knew they weren't talking about checkers but about the intricacies involving a male and female.

But was she willing to learn?

Chance lay in bed and could only stare up at the ceiling as he heard the shower going, imagining Kylie, naked and standing beneath a full spray of water that flowed down her breasts, flat stomach, thighs…

He tried tuning out the sound and turning his attention to his snoring son, who was sleeping on the opposite bunk. Damn, he sounded just like Donovan. Chance chuckled as he remembered that while growing up no one wanted to share a bedroom with Donovan because he snored.

After a few moments he released a groan and decided listening to Kylie in the shower was a lot better than putting up with Marcus. He smiled, thinking he had really enjoyed their conversation on the porch tonight. She seemed interested in his family, which was just as well, since if he had his way the Steeles would be her family one day.

God, he loved her.

Heat sizzled along his nerve endings at the thought of just how much. A slow, sinful grin touched his lips when he thought about what he'd told her last night. There was a lot she didn't understand about man-woman relationships and he intended to teach her. Things had definitely changed since her last date, especially in the bedroom. If he remembered correctly, that was the year the Hubble Telescope was launched into space, Nelson Mandela was finally freed from prison and George Bush Senior was president.

Hell, she probably wasn't aware that these days men and women who were in a serious relationship openly discussed such things as foreplay and orgasms, or that trying different positions in the bedroom was now the norm and not the exception. And she'd probably be startled to know that oral sex was pretty popular these days.

A slow smile rolled around his lips. Yes, he would enjoy teaching her all the finer things in life with one goal in mind: to make her fall as deeply in love with him as he was with her.

Chapter 9

"Well, Lena, how do I look?"

Lena stood with her hands on her hips and gave Kylie an assessing stare. The two of them had been shopping for gowns to wear to this weekend's ball and it seemed as if Kylie had hit the jackpot.

"Girl, that dress is gorgeous and it looks fabulous on you," Lena said. "But of course you have the figure for it. You have more curves than the Daytona Speedway. You'd be nuts not to buy it."

With her courage bolstered, Kylie looked down at herself. Lena was right. The dress was a sexy black form-fitting georgette mini with a halter criss-cross bodice and a low-cut back. She had to admit it did look rather flattering on her, though it showed more skin than she would like.

"You don't think it's too daring?" she asked Lena.

"Heck, no, like I said you have the body for it. Everyone can't say that. I most certainly can't."

Kylie frowned at her friend. "Hey, there's nothing wrong with your figure."

"That losing fifteen more pounds won't hurt?"

"Don't complain. A lot of men like full-figured women. You have a small waist, nice size hips, a gorgeous pair of legs—"

"Strong bones and a good set of teeth," Lena tagged on. They laughed, remembering other times they had gone shopping together when they were much younger and faced with the same dilemma. Kylie always thought she was too thin and Lena had made up in her mind years ago that at size sixteen she was too thick.

"So, are you going to buy it?" Lena asked as she walked around Kylie, admiring how the dress fit.

"Probably not," Kylie said, still looking down at herself. She felt half-naked wearing it. "But it's gorgeous, though."

"And it has your name on it."

Kylie glanced up at Lena. "You think so?"

"I wouldn't have said it if I didn't. Besides, since you've decided to be my date for the ball what I say counts, right?"

"Right."

"So what are you going to do?"

Kylie grinned. "I'm going to take it."

An hour or so later they were back in Lena's car and exiting the mall. "You never told me how things went last weekend with the camping trip," Lena said.

Kylie glanced over at her. "Didn't think I had to. I'm sure Tiffany told you everything you needed to know."

"Yeah, but she didn't mention anything about you and Chance."

"Was she supposed to?"

"I guess not, if the two of you are keeping your affair a secret."

Kylie gave her friend a direct stare, although Lena's eyes were glued to the road and didn't notice it. "Chance and I are not having an affair."

"Oh. The two of you just meet every so often to lock lips, right?"

Kylie rolled her eyes heavenward. "So, we kissed a few times, no big deal."

"I would think after fifteen years of abstinence that for you it *was* a big deal. And you even admitted he was a good kisser."

"Oh, my gosh, he's the best," Kylie breathed and then regretted that she'd admitted it.

Lena laughed. "Bingo. So how did you manage to keep those overzealous hormones under control?"

"It was hard but I managed."

"And the two of you didn't kiss not even once?"

"No, not even once. Marcus and Tiffany kept us much too busy. They wanted to do everything and by the end of the day we were too tired to do anything but sleep."

"Oh, how sad."

Lena and Kylie looked at each other and burst out laughing again. A few moments later, Lena said, "You know he's coming to the ball, don't you?"

Kylie tried to keep her attention on an object outside of the car's window. "What Chance does is his business."

"And he's bringing a date."

Kylie jerked her head around. "What!"

Lena laughed out loud. "Gotcha!"

Kylie frowned. "That's not funny, Lena."

"It is, too. You should have seen the way your head snapped around. It's a wonder you didn't break your neck. For someone who claims what Chance Steele does is his business, you were definitely interested in that piece of news."

"Well, is it true? Is he bringing someone?"

Lena shrugged. "Don't know. Cassandra Tisdale mentioned at committee meeting yesterday that her cousin was going to be in town that night from D.C. and she was going to ask Chance to be the woman's date."

"Good for her."

"Umm, do I detect a little jealousy in your voice?"

"Not on your life."

Lena smiled. "Okay, if you say so."

Lena was right, Kylie thought as she got ready for bed that night. She was jealous. Of all the nerve!

She had to admit that Chance had been on his best behavior last weekend, probably because she didn't give him the chance to be otherwise. After that first night when he had invited her to sit out on the porch with him, she had gotten smart and made sure the opportunity never presented itself again. She went to bed when Tiffany went to bed and she stayed there.

Still, she thought things had gone rather well that weekend and Marcus and Chance had been perfect hosts. They had seen to all of her and Tiffany's needs, and with Tiffany and Marcus carrying on more like siblings instead of a couple the majority of the time, it was as if the four of them were a family.

Chance had been wonderful with Tiffany when he showed her the proper way to use a rod and reel, after Marcus had thrown up his hands and given up. And then there was the time Chance taught Tiffany how to paddle the canoe, and how he was the only one who actually seemed interested in her obsession with bird-watching. Seeing them together actually made her wonder if perhaps Tiffany had lost out by not having a father figure in her life all these years. At least Tiffany would have the chance to spend time with her grandfather this weekend. Kylie's parents had called a few days ago and asked if Tiffany could go with them to Disney World for the weekend.

Since both Friday and the following Monday were teachers' planning days, things worked out perfectly. Kylie would put her on the plane Friday morning and then pick her up from the airport on Monday evening. That meant she wouldn't have to worry about her daughter while she attended this weekend's ball.

The phone rang and Kylie glanced over at the

clock, knowing it was Chance. How could he talk to her every night and not mention he was taking someone to the ball? It didn't matter to her one iota that she hadn't taken Lena's advice and invited him herself. It was the principle of the thing.

She frowned when she picked up the phone. "Hello."

"How did things go at work today?"

This was how they began their conversation each night. He would ask her how things went with her job and she would ask how things went with his. They would hold a pleasant conversation for a good forty-five minutes and then they would say good night. Sometimes she wondered about the real purpose of them talking, other than to hear the other's voice each day.

"Things at the shop went okay. Business has really picked up this week. I got a lot of pre-Thanksgiving orders." Then she said, "I closed early. Lena and I went shopping for gowns for the ball this weekend." She wondered if he would mention if he were going, or more specifically if he had a date.

"Did you find something you liked?"

"Yes."

"What color is it?"

"Black."

"I bet it looks good on you."

"Lena thought so."

"Did she?"

"Yes."

There was a pause and then he said, "Marcus is going away this weekend."

Kylie raised an eyebrow. This was news to her since Tiffany hadn't mentioned it. "He is?"

"Yes. Cyndi's parents are coming through on their way to—"

"Not Disney World?" she asked, immediately jumping to conclusions and hoping they were the wrong ones.

"No, Busch Gardens in Virginia."

Thank goodness. "Oh."

"Why did you think they were going to Disney World?"

"Because that's where Tiffany is headed this weekend."

"Ahh. And you thought that perhaps they had ma-nipulated their grandparents so the two of them could be in the same place and at the same time."

"It's been known to happen."

"I'm sure it has but I doubt they would go that far."

"Hey, you never know," Kylie said.

There was another pause and then Chance said, "We're going to have to start trusting them at some point, Kylie."

Tucking a braid behind her ear, she took a deep, frustrating breath. "I know but for me it's hard, Chance, because I remember all the tricks I used to pull to be with Sam."

"Yes, but is it fair to judge them by what you did?"

"No."

"All right, then."

Kylie tilted her lips in a smile. Even if he were bringing a date to the ball, she still enjoyed her nightly talks with him. Although she had decided that they could never be lovers, it seemed that he had made up his mind that they would be friends. And deep down she didn't have a problem with that.

She'd always had Lena as another female to bounce her ideas and thoughts off of, but there had never been a guy she felt close enough with to do the same. Lately she had asked Chance's opinions about a lot things, including how she should handle situations that had arisen at work. Being the savvy businessman that he was, he had always given her good, sound advice.

"So, how are things going at the Steele Corporation?" she asked.

"There was a development today that I wished could have been avoided."

"Oh? What?"

"We had to let a man go who's been with us for over ten years."

She heard disappointment, as well as regret, in his voice. "Why?"

"We found out he'd been stealing from the company. He was padding figures and having the products delivered elsewhere. Bas had suspected him for a while but we only got the proof we needed today to do anything about it."

They talked for the next thirty minutes or so and that night Kylie slept with an inner peace that she hadn't known in a long time.

"So you think they will have their first date this weekend?" Marcus asked before biting into his sandwich.

Tiffany smiled. "Yes. They're going to that ball although they aren't going with each other. I can't see how it won't turn into a date with the both of us gone for the weekend. Didn't you see how they were looking at each other last weekend when they thought no one was noticing? I think we did the right thing by contacting our grandparents."

Marcus nodded. "I hope you're right."

Tiffany took another sip of her soda, smiled and said, "Just think, Marcus, if we actually pull this off, you'll be the big brother I've always wanted."

Marcus grinned. "Yeah, and then I can give Rhonda Denton my full attention. I think she likes me."

Chapter 10

*H*e wanted her.

That thought rammed through Chance's mind the moment he saw Kylie enter the ballroom. His heart began hammering in his chest and he actually felt his pulse rate spike drastically. And if that wasn't bad enough, his body got hard as a rock.

At that moment he was grateful he was standing behind a waist-high plant that could shield the physical evidence of just how much he desired her. That, coupled with the knowledge of how much he loved her, was setting his loins on fire.

The minidress she was wearing was definitely a shocker he could sum up in three words—short, sassy and sexy. It fit her body to perfection, showing off all her curves and the luscious length of her long, shapely legs. And if the dress wasn't jaw-droppingly seductive enough, then there was the way she had her hair piled atop her head with a few swirling braids crowning her face.

"Who are they?" Morgan leaned over and whispered, while raising an impressive eyebrow. "I don't know either of them," he said as if it were his God-given right to be acquainted with every beautiful woman in Charlotte.

Chance studied his brother's face for a second and noted his gaze wasn't as glued to Kylie as it was to Lena Spears. That was a good thing since it would have been of waste of Morgan's time to show any interest in Kylie. When it came to her he could get downright territorial. "The one in the black dress is Kylie Hagan, and she's mine," he said, deciding to state his claim here and now. "The woman in the fuchsia dress is her best friend, Lena Spears."

"Spears? Where have I heard that name before?" Morgan asked.

"I have no idea. She's a part of the committee

that put on tonight's ball and owns a real estate office in town."

"A real estate office?"

"Yes."

Morgan glanced over at Chance after taking a sip from his wineglass. "You know her, then?"

"Yes."

Morgan's dark eyes sparkled in the glow of the huge chandelier that hung over their heads. "Good. I want an introduction." He then glanced back over at the two women. "So the one in black is Marcus's girlfriend's mother?"

At Chance's nod, he said, "Umm, definitely good-looking. But she doesn't look old enough to have a fifteen-year-old daughter."

"Well, she does," Chance answered, with no intention of going into any details as to how that had happened.

For a brief moment Morgan didn't say anything and then he spoke. "It seems she's caught Derek Peterson's eye. He didn't waste any time going over there to talk to her. If I were you I'd go claim what's mine."

Chance had noticed the man's flight across to the room to get all in Kylie's face. Derek Peterson, twice divorced, had a reputation as a skirt chaser and it seemed that he wasn't wasting any time making Kylie's acquaintance. "I think I will."

"Aren't you going to introduce me to your friend, Lena?" Derek Peterson asked.

"I'll think about it," Lena responded noncommittally.

Kylie raised an eyebrow. Lena was known for her friendly disposition. If she was giving this man the cold shoulder, there must be a good reason.

"Since Lena won't cooperate, I guess I have to introduce myself," the man said, capturing Kylie's hand in his. "I'm Dr. Derek Peterson."

Upon recognizing the name, Kylie understood her friend's less-than-friendly attitude. Derek was a doctor who had at one time shown interest in Lena until he discovered she was her elderly mother's caretaker. He'd told her there was no way the two of them could get serious since she came with "extra baggage."

"And I'm Kylie Hagan," Kylie said, in an attempt to be polite.

He gave her a smile that showed perfect white teeth. "Ms. Hagan, it is a pleasure to meet you. You must be new to town."

Kylie decided she didn't like him any more than

Lena did, probably because his gaze was focused more on her chest than her face. "I've been living here for almost four months now."

"What section of town do you live in?"

"Myers Park."

"Myers Park?"

"Yes." She heard his impressed tone. Myers Park, one of the first suburbs of Charlotte, featured large stately homes that were canopied in willow oaks. More than any other neighborhood in the city, Myers Park had preserved its true character over the years. The "front-porch" neighborhoods had the traditional sidewalks, funky shops and restaurants. The house she had purchased had cost a pretty penny but thanks to Lena's negotiating skills, the owners, who'd needed a quick sale, had readily agreed to her offer.

"Then I must definitely get to know you. We're neighbors," Dr. Peterson said, "though I don't ever remember running into you while out and about."

Kylie was just about to tell him that she was both a fulltime mother and a working woman who didn't have time to be "out and about," when she felt a sudden quiver in her midsection. She knew without a doubt that Chance was in close range.

She didn't want to seem too obvious when she scanned the crowded ballroom, but knew from the way her heart began hammering that she didn't have to look far. He stood on a raised dais, staring directly at her. The person standing by his side was a man and not a woman, which gave her some relief. It was easy to tell the man was one of his brothers, as the resemblance was striking.

What was also obvious was the intensity in Chance's eyes. She could almost drown in the look she saw there. Male interest. Male appreciation. Male longing. Even a novice like her could recognize the three. He was silently sending her a message, one her body fully understood. Her hormones were on ready, set, go. But she knew there was something else involved here; something she hadn't counted on happening. It was also something she wasn't prepared for.

Emotional feelings of the deepest kind.

Now she understood why she'd been having all those vibrant and uncontrollable urges since meeting Chance. And why her body was so aware of him whether he was with her in person or was talking to her on the phone. The thought that he easily ignited her fire had always bothered her because she hadn't understood the why of it. Whenever he kissed her she got caught up in his special skill of tongue-play, as if his tongue was made for her and hers for him. She hadn't wanted to get in the same fix she'd been in with Sam; something she now thought of as forbidden obsession.

She was old enough now to know better. She was at that age of maturity where she no longer took things at face value. She didn't trust easily and had a tendency to expect the worst. But standing here being absorbed in Chance's heated gaze she knew at that moment that it wasn't about obsession, nor was it about lust. It was about love.

She had fallen head over heels in love with him.

"And what do you do for a living, Kylie?"

She tore her gaze away from Chance upon hearing Dr. Peterson's question. "I own a florist shop."

"Oh? Where?"

"In the newly developed section of town, Hazelwood."

"That's a nice area, but if you ever want to move to another location, a friend of mine owns a couple of buildings that he's leasing downtown and—"

"Good evening, everyone."

That deep, husky voice made the pounding of Kylie's heart increase. She glanced up and met Chance's direct gaze.

"Chance! It's good to see you," Lena said, deliberately showing a lot more enthusiasm upon seeing him than she had Dr. Peterson.

"Thanks, Lena, and it's good seeing you as well."

He then gazed back at Kylie and held out his hand. "Hello, I'm Chance Steele. And you're...?"

Kylie wondered what game Chance was playing, but at the moment deciding to go along with him. "Kylie Hagan."

"Well, Ms. Hagan, it's nice meeting you. And I'd like to introduce my brother, Morgan." He then proceeded to introduce Morgan Steele to both her and Lena. It was only then that she noted that he'd given Derek no more than a cursory glance. Kylie immediately felt the tension that surrounded the three men and was bewildered by it.

"Derek," Chance acknowledged.

"Chance. Morgan. I thought you guys ran in packs. Where're the other two?"

Chance's smile didn't quite reach his eyes. "Bas and Donovan are around here somewhere. Why? Are you looking for them?"

"No." Derek then turned his attention to Kylie. "It was nice meeting you, Ms. Hagan, but I'm being beckoned elsewhere."

"And it was nice meeting you as well, Dr. Peterson." The man quickly left. Once he was no longer in sight, Kylie turned to Chance to inquire what that had been about, but found her hand enveloped in the warmth of his when the orchestra began playing.

She met his gaze and all thoughts of Derek Peterson were forgotten as she was immediately swept away by the intensity in Chance's dark eyes and the warmth of the smile that spread across his features. "Would you dance with me?" he asked quietly.

She wondered if he could sense her inner turmoil. Did he know the emotions she was feeling were real and far exceeded the ones she'd assumed she had felt for Sam all those years ago? What she'd felt then was the passion of a young, naive girl. What she was experiencing now was the passion of an adult woman who had discovered love for the first time and knew there was no place for her to run, and no place for her to hide. There was nothing she could do but accept her fate.

Love was staring her in the face in the form of Chance Marcus Steele.

"Yes, I'll dance with you." His hand on hers tightened gently and she felt the warm strength of his touch as he led her toward the dance floor.

Once there he pulled her into his arms, close to the solidness of his form, the heat of his body. She wondered how long she could continue to stand and not melt at his feet with all the sensations overtaking her. Finding out at thirty-one that you had the ability to love again was definitely a shocker.

"You look beautiful tonight, Kylie," Chance said, claiming her absolute attention. "Without a doubt you are the most gorgeous woman here."

Kylie lowered her gaze to study the Rolex watch on his wrist. "Your date might have a problem with you thinking that."

"I didn't bring a date."

She raised surprised eyes to his. "You didn't?"

"No. What made you think I did? Or even more important, what made you think I would?"

"Your brother's fiancée mentioned to Lena that some woman in her family was coming to town and that you would be bringing her to the ball."

He shrugged. "Cassandra did call and try convincing me to escort her cousin tonight but I refused."

"Why?" she asked swiftly, then regretted doing so. It was really none of her business.

"Because the only woman I want to be with tonight was going to be here, although she didn't ask me to be her date."

Kylie couldn't help but smile, elated he'd come alone. "Oh, what a pity," she commented teasingly.

"Yes, I thought so as well. But now that she's here, right where I want her to be, which is in my arms, I'm declaring myself her date for the rest of the night."

Kylie didn't have a problem with that. "Are you?"

"Yes. That's one sure way to protect you from the Derek Petersons of the world."

The contempt she heard in his voice proved her earlier assumption had been correct. There was no love lost between Derek, Chance and Morgan. "You and Morgan don't like him," she said, stating what had been so obvious. "Why?"

"Let's just say we don't exactly appreciate the way he's been known to treat women."

Not wanting to talk about Derek Peterson any longer, Chance brought Kylie's body closer to his. He drank in her softness, her nearness, her scent—everything that was woman about her. After seven years of doing without a woman in his life, the one he was holding in his arms made him feel complete.

"Why did you pretend that the two of us hadn't met before?"

Kylie's question invaded Chance's thoughts. He gazed at her, thinking that her question was easy enough to answer. "Something you said a few weeks ago made me want to prove you wrong."

She arched an eyebrow. "And what did I say?"

"You said that we had only met because of our kids and chances were if we'd been at any function together that I would not have given you a second look. It was your opinion that you're not the type of woman I would have shown interest in."

Kylie nodded, remembering she *had* said that. "And?"

"And I've proven you wrong, Kylie," he drawled. She gave him a bemused look. "How?"

"By being here with you tonight, seeing you walk through that door for the first time. Tonight has nothing to do with our kids. It's a function where we are both in attendance, and I did give you a second look. You are definitely a woman I would be interested in. And to go even further, you *are* a woman I *am* interested in, Kylie. The *only* one I'm interested in."

His words touched her more than he would ever know and Kylie didn't think she could feel more desired and more wanted than at that very moment. The way he was looking at her made her feel hot, feverish. The intensity in his eyes made her pulse flutter and a heat wave consumed her, sending blood thrumming through her veins. She felt her nipples puckering against his chest. What was passing between them was too arousing for a dance floor.

The music ended and she felt him curl his fingers around her upper arm to lead her toward the exit doors. "Where are we going?" she asked breathlessly, trying to keep up with his long strides.

"Outside to get some fresh air."

Kylie swallowed. She had a feeling that fresh air wasn't the only thing Chance intended to get.

When Chance finally came to a stop beneath a cascade of low-hanging branches, he turned to Kylie and gently pulled her to him. And when his lips creased into that sexy smile that could automatically turn her on, she didn't think twice about tilting her head back for his kiss.

Her breath escaped in a shallow sigh the moment he slanted his mouth across hers, causing her already heated body to become a blazing flame. And when the glide of his tongue across hers caused her stomach to clench, she reached up and wound her arms around his neck, bringing their bodies closer.

She felt his erection pressed so strongly against her, actually wedged between her thighs, and moaned in his mouth at the same time her body instinctively rocked against him. A part of her didn't know what to make of her actions. She had never been this loose, this free with any man. The couple of times she and Sam had made out, she'd been too busy worrying about whether they would get caught to fully enjoy the experience.

Now getting caught was the last thing on her mind. If an entire ballroom discovered her and Chance outside kissing beneath a bunch of willow branches, then so be it. Nothing, and she meant nothing, could make her stop being a participant in this. She'd needed his mouth on hers, his seductive taste mingling with her own tongue more than she had known. She had been hungry and now he was feeding her with a skill that only he possessed. He tasted, stroked and tangled his way around her mouth, pleasuring her as only he could do.

And then she felt him smooth a hand up her silken thigh. As it eased beneath her short dress and inched its way to her waist, she moaned deep within her throat. The sensations his touch invoked overwhelmed her and instinctively she arched closer to him.

Slowly he released her mouth, raised his head and met her gaze, and she knew he saw the longing that was there in the dark depths of her eyes, mirroring what she saw in his. He reached up and skimmed a fingertip across her lips and she moaned against his finger. Heat shot down to the area between her legs.

"I want to leave here and take you somewhere to be alone with you, Kylie."

She knew what he was asking. She knew what he was saying. He might not love her but he wanted her. And at that moment it was all that mattered to her. What he'd tried telling her all along suddenly made perfect sense. They were adults and they could do whatever they wanted to do within reason. Would it be so awful to take what he was offering? A chance for the two of them to be alone? She had lived the past fifteen years without a man in her life, she didn't need promises of forever.

Right now the only thing she needed was him, the man she knew she loved. And for the first time in a very long time, she would be led by her heart and not her mind. Regrets, if there were any, could come later.

"I want to be alone with you, too, Chance."

"I'm glad to hear that," he whispered, smiling. "I think we should go back inside, mingle, dance a couple more times and then leave. What do you think of that?"

She smiled up at him. The thought of being alone with him later made her heart beat in an erratic rhythm, and the pure male desire shimmering in his eyes wasn't helping matters. "I think that's a wonderful idea."

The moment they stepped back into the ballroom a woman called out to Chance, claiming his attention. They turned and watched two beautiful, and gorgeously dressed women head their way. Chance's hand on Kylie's arm tightened and when she glanced up at him she could detect a frown that he was trying to hide behind a forced smile.

"Chance, I've been looking for you."

"Hello, Cassandra. I'd like you to meet a friend of mine, Kylie Hagan."

Cassandra barely spared Kylie a glance, until she noticed Chance's hand possessively on her arm. Then, after a swift appraisal, she extended her hand. "Oh, hello. Have we met before?"

"I don't think so," Kylie said, noticing the woman's immediate dislike of her. The feeling was reciprocal.

Cassandra then turned her attention back to Chance and to the woman at her side. "This is my cousin, Jamie, the one I told you about who's visiting from Washington, D.C."

"Hello, Jamie. Welcome to Charlotte," Chance said politely. He then turned to Kylie. "And, Jamie, I'd like you to meet Kylie Hagan, a good friend."

After introductions were made Cassandra didn't waste time. "Chance, I think you and Jamie should spend time together while she's in town," she said, disregarding Kylie and Chance's hold on her arm.

"Really? And why would you think that?"

"Because her father is Senator Hollis."

Chance's expression became barely tolerant. It appeared he didn't appreciate Cassandra's lack of manners. "Sorry, but is that supposed to mean something to me?"

Cassandra tilted her head back to look at him. The glint in her eyes said she was annoyed. "Well, I thought it would since you're a businessman interested in world trade and he's on the Fair Trade Commission in Washington."

"Well, that's all rather nice," Chance said, irritation evident in his tone. "But I don't think I need Jamie to arrange a meeting with her father if I ever need to discuss business with him. After all, he is a paid politician representing *all* the people, right?"

Cassandra's hazel eyes narrowed. "Right."

"Okay, then." In an attempt to save face, he changed the subject. "The committee did a wonderful job with the ball tonight, Cassandra. Kylie and I were headed over to the buffet table."

"Well, enjoy," Cassandra said, clearly not happy that she hadn't gotten Chance to bend her way.

Chance gave Jamie a smile. "It was nice meeting

you. Give your father my regards." Tightening his hold on Kylie's arm, they walked off.

When they reached the buffet table, Chance let out a long sigh. "That woman had a lot of nerve to suggest that I date her cousin while you were standing there. She was willing to use Jamie's father's political connection to set her up on a date. I've never seen anything so tacky. I'm sorry about that."

Kylie chuckled as she picked up a plate. "Don't be. I learned a long time ago that usually it's people with money who lack real manners."

"I hope you're not grouping everyone with money in that category."

She smiled up at him. "No, only some of them. The Cassandras and the Dereks of this world."

Chance grinned. "I agree."

They remained at the ball for an additional hour or so, long enough to mingle and for Kylie to meet Chance's three female cousins, and his other two brothers, whom she thought were as handsome and as well-mannered as Chance and Morgan. After meeting Sebastian Steele, she couldn't picture him married to someone like Cassandra Tisdale.

"We've hung around long enough," Chance whispered in her ear. "Ready to leave?"

She looked up at him, her smoldering eyes telling him she'd been anxiously counting the minutes. "Yes, I'm ready."

They left the ball, then waited as a valet brought Chance's car to them. It was then that he asked, "Did you need to find Lena and let her know you've left with me?"

She shook her head. "I think she'll have an idea what happened when she doesn't see me anymore tonight."

He opened the passenger door on his car when it came. "Will her knowing bother you?"

"No. Will her knowing bother you?"

"No."

"What about your brothers and cousins?" she asked.

"It wouldn't bother me for anyone to know we're together, Kylie," he said, closing the door when she slid onto the smooth leather seat.

When he got inside the vehicle and slid beneath the steering wheel she said, "Nice car."

He grinned. "Thanks. I decided to leave the truck home and bring my toy."

She chuckled. A Mercedes sports car was some toy. "Where are we going?"

He glanced over at her. "Where do you want to go?"

They could go to either her place or his since there weren't any kids at home. That thought made a girlish giggle escape her lips. He glanced over at her when he pulled out of the parking lot and headed toward the interstate. "Are you okay?"

She grinned. "Yes. I was just thinking that with the kids away the parents will play. I feel like being naughty tonight, Chance."

He surprised her when he braked and veered off to the shoulder of the road.

"Why are we stopping, Chance?"

"I feel like being naughty tonight too, starting now," he replied simply, before leaning over and connecting her mouth with his again. Her lips parted without any hesitation and his aggressive tongue mingled diligently with hers. He tasted of the wine he had consumed earlier and it only raised her body's temperature. She returned his intensity with her own, and as their tongues mingled, her insides turned to molten liquid.

When he pulled back, they were both breathless. He captured her gaze, held it. "So, will it be my place or yours?"

She reached out and placed her palm against his cheek. "Mine. I want you in *my* bed, Chance Steele."

Chapter 11

Less than a half hour later, they entered Kylie's home. As she closed the door, a warm, tingly, tantalizing sensation began building up inside of her in anticipation of what was to come.

There in the middle of the room stood Chance. The dark eyes looking at her were smoldering and, as always, he looked the embodiment of extreme male sexuality. And there was no doubt that he was the most tempting sight she'd ever seen.

Neither of them spoke.

He continued to look at her, long and hard,

making her already heated body that much hotter, making her fully aroused. When she thought there was no way she could stand the intensity of his gaze any longer, he smiled, that slow, sexy smile that was meant to warm her. Instead it ignited everything woman within her, making her body respond to his physical presence in the most primitive way. When she thought she couldn't possibly take any more, he slowly closed the distance separating them.

"Are you sure about this, Kylie?" he whispered huskily, taking her hand in his and bringing her closer to him. So close that she felt his huge erection.

Kylie felt off balance and her mind became a mass of desire, of wanting, of need. "I've never been so sure of anything in my life, Chance," she whispered back. "But…"

"But what?"

"But I don't have any real experience at this and I don't want to disappoint you."

He wrapped his arms around her waist and pulled her closer still. "Trust me, sweetheart, you won't. There's no way you can."

He leaned down and took her lips, and seconds later she felt herself being lifted in his strong arms. He carried her up the stairs. "Which room is yours?" he asked when he'd reached the landing.

"The first door to your right."

She had left a low lamp burning in her bedroom and now it cast an intimate glow in the room.

"I love that dress you have on but it's coming off, Kylie," he said as he set her on her feet. Without hesitation he stripped off his tuxedo jacket and bow tie, and unbuttoned his white shirt.

She tilted her head back. "If you want it off, you'll have to take it off," she said with sass.

He accepted the sensuous challenge in her voice. "I have no problem doing that, because it *is* coming off. I have a lot of plans for you tonight."

She smiled. Whether he knew it or not, she had a lot of plans for him as well. "I take it you're going to teach me a few things."

"Yes," he said, undoing the last of his buttons, exposing his muscular chest. She had seen his chest before, when they'd gone camping and he had taken a swim in the lake. And then, like now, she thought it was definitely a chest worth looking at, worth sliding her hands over, worth teasing with her tongue.

Her gaze followed Chance's fingers as he removed his shirt and tossed it aside, but when those same fingers went to the fastener of his pants her breath caught. Still, she couldn't avert her eyes. They watched as he eased his zipper down. A heaviness settled in her stomach and every nerve ending within her came vibrantly alive when he pushed those same pants down his hips.

She had never seen a man undress before. At sixteen she had actually closed her eyes when Sam had done it. As an adult she was now seeing a male in the flesh for the first time. She'd always suspected Chance had a nice body, but now, she saw first hand just how nice it was. And she saw just how aroused he was since the black briefs he wore showed the large ridge of his erection. She couldn't help but stare when he proceeded to remove the last stitch of clothing.

"Now it's time for your clothes to come off."

Her gaze flew up to his face, fighting the panic of not knowing just how her body would be able to accommodate such a well-endowed man. But when her eyes met his, that sexy smile of his aroused her even more and she knew that she wouldn't worry. The two of them would fit perfectly.

With slow and precise steps, he covered the short distance separating them and his hand, as gentle as it could be, reached out and stroked her arm. "Do you know how often I've dreamed about undressing you?" he whispered huskily as he lifted her hand to his mouth and kissed her palm.

She took a deep breath to steady herself. The touch of his moist tongue on her hand only fueled the fire that was steadily burning inside of her. "No, how often?" she managed to get out in a raspy breath.

"Too often," he said, reaching behind her to undo the clasp at the nape of her neck. "And seeing you in this dress tonight didn't help matters any."

He took a step back, loosened the straps away from her neck and the black georgette material slid down her legs. And when he offered her his hand for assistance, she took it and stepped out of the dress. Now she was naked except for her thong, thigh-high hose and shoes.

His gaze, she noticed, was fastened on her breasts and she watched, as if in slow motion, when he reached out and fondled them, caressing them, shaping them to the feel of his hands.

At his touch, her breathing became erratic, and she leaned into him to grip his shoulders, for fear she would melt to the floor. She clutched him when he leaned forward and took a nipple into his mouth, licking and sucking first one then the other. Each and every tug sent sensuous sensations all the way to her womb.

"Chance," she whispered, arching toward him

even more. She gasped when he scooped her into his arms and carried her over to the bed, placed her on it. Gently he removed her shoes and then his hand slid up her legs to get rid of her hose. Taking off her thong was easy since there wasn't much to it but Kylie saw how dark his eyes got when the most intimate part of her body became exposed.

His smoldering gaze focused on the mound between her thighs, and Kylie began to feel nervous with all the attention. Chance was definitely enjoying the view, but if he only knew how fast her heart was beating, he wouldn't be looking at her this way.

"I want you, Kylie," he said silkily.

She met his gaze and replied softly, "I want you, too, Chance."

Her words, spoken honestly and seductively, zapped Chance of what little control he had. Placing a knee on the bed, he reached down and drew her naked body to his and kissed her with all the love he had in his heart. The moment he slipped his tongue inside her mouth she latched on to it, returning his kiss with an intensity he knew the both of them felt.

He reluctantly broke the kiss and began caressing her all over, becoming familiar with the soft feel of her body and the sexy scent of her arousal. He kissed her all over, starting with her breasts and moving down to her navel, but as he went lower still, he felt her tense. Knowing he was about to carry her through unchartered waters, he lifted his head and met her gaze. "Kylie?"

The eyes that met his were glazed with desire and shadowed in uncertainty. "Yes?"

"Do you trust me?"

"Yes," she responded in a breathy sound. "I trust you."

"How much?" he asked, giving her one of those sexy smiles again.

Her voice was soft and throaty when she said, "Considering all you know about me, I trust you a lot. I haven't been with anyone in fifteen years, Chance. That in itself should say something."

"It does. And your trust in me is special. I want to make not just tonight, but this entire weekend special for the both of us."

He must have read the question in her eyes, as he chuckled and said. "And no, I don't plan on keeping you in bed all weekend. There's going to be more to our relationship than sex, Kylie. I want to take you on our first official date tomorrow night. Will you let me do that?"

Kylie caught her bottom lip between her teeth.

She still wasn't ready for their kids to know they were involved, but with Marcus and Tiffany away for the weekend, she and Chance were finally free to do whatever they wanted to do. "Yes, I'd like that," she said quietly.

He smiled. "Good. And another thing."

She quirked an eyebrow. "What?"

"I want to introduce you to various types of love-making but I promise to take things slow and easy. And I also promise not to do anything you're not comfortable with doing. I want to show you that making love is the most intimate act two people can share, as well as the most pleasurable. And I want to share every aspect of it with you." He reached out his hand and slowly traced it up her leg toward the center of her thighs.

The closer he got to a certain part of her, the harder it became for Kylie to concentrate and to breathe. "Every aspect?" she asked breathlessly.

"Yes. I want to take you to a place you've never been before. Pleasureland. I want us to go there together and participate in the kind of pleasure that only the two of us can generate." His voice went lower when he asked, "Will you go there with me?"

She swallowed when his knuckles nudged her thighs apart and his fingers touched her—right there in what had to be her hot spot. And she knew he'd found her not only hot but wet as well. "Yes, I'll go there with you," she said, barely able to get the words out.

"Anyplace? At anytime…within reason?"

Chance was stroking her and she could feel pressure building inside of her. Pressure she needed to release. "Yes."

"My touching you this way is just the beginning," he said as he continued to stroke her. "I want to take you on one hell of an adventure. Are you okay with that?"

Biting back a moan, she closed her eyes. "Yes, I'm okay with it." The feathery touch of his fingers was slowly driving her insane. It seemed as if he was touching every sensitive cell that was located between her legs.

"You sure?"

"Yes, I'm sure."

"And what if I replaced my fingers with my tongue?" he leaned over and whispered hotly in her ear.

Her eyes flew open. And she knew the flush that had suddenly appeared on her face told him everything. She took a deep breath as she melted inside with the thought of him doing that. "Why would you want to do that?" she somehow managed to ask.

"Because I want to satisfy my taste for you in a way that kissing won't do, Kylie."

"But no one has ever…I've never . . ."

"Yes, I know," he said silkily. "But I want to be your first. May I?"

Her heart pounded erratically in her chest. She had to swallow twice before she spoke. "Yes, if you're sure you want to do that."

"Oh, baby, more than anything, I do."

As soon as he had spoken those words, Chance slid off the bed, gently brought her body closer to the edge and knelt in front of her open legs. Then he leaned forward, inhaled her scent and took her into his mouth.

Kylie's body bucked at the first touch of his tongue. A deep groan escaped her throat when he proceeded to taste her with a hunger that appeared unquenched. She clutched the bedspread, needing something to hold on to. His mouth was literally driving her insane and she had to clamp her lips closed to stop herself from screaming.

Chance lifted his mouth only long enough to say, "Just let go, baby, and come for me."

No sooner had he replaced his mouth on her, she did just what he had asked. The force of the climax hit her. And when it did she forgot everything except how all of her senses seemed to be gathered at this one particular spot, making it impossible to hold back. She screamed out his name when her body splintered into a thousand pieces. Waves and waves of pleasure washed over her and through her. She cried out several more times as her body, soul and mind were transported to a place where only pleasure resided.

Pleasureland.

It was a place that only Chance could take her.

Chance reluctantly pulled his mouth away and sat back on his heels, watching the last contractions of Kylie's orgasm move through her. He had dreamed of taking her this way for so long, the only thing he could do for the moment was to sit there and inhale the womanly scent of her, savor her taste.

Hearing the woman he loved scream out his name had filled him with a joy he'd never felt before. But he knew for them, this was just the beginning of one hell of a weekend, one hell of a relationship, and one hell of a future.

Driven by an intense need to become a part of her in yet another way, he reached for the pants he had discarded earlier. He pulled his wallet out of the back pocket to get one of the condoms he'd put there.

He quickly slipped it on, wanting to join their bodies while she was still in the throes of lingering passion.

He eased her back to the center of the bed and joined her there. When his face was mere inches from hers she slowly opened her eyes and met his gaze. A satisfied curve touched the corners of her mouth. "Hi."

He smiled back. "Hi."

"I came," she said like it had been a miracle, a pleasure she would remember always.

He smiled. "Yes, you did and I'm going to make you come again."

She blinked at him as if such a thing wasn't possible. "You will," he assured her.

And then he kissed her, taking her mouth in a way that let her know just how intent he was on making it happen for her again. Moments later, his mouth left hers to skim down her jaw, past her neck, as it traced a damp trail toward her breasts, tasting them as he'd done earlier, while reaching down to sink his fingers in the flesh he had just tasted awhile ago.

"Chance." She called out his name when she felt her body getting all heated again.

He eased over her. "Open your eyes, Kylie, and look at me." He wanted to be caught in her gaze the exact moment he joined with her. If she wasn't quite ready to hear about his love, he wanted her to at least feel it.

Desire and love pulsed through his veins, made his erection just that much harder, thicker, and when she opened her eyes he knew he needed to be inside of her, feel the length of him stroking her, claiming her as his, totally consuming her.

He raised her hands above her head and with their fingers laced together, their gazes locked, he slowly eased inside of her, finding her wet, ready, yet tight.

"Oh, Chance. I need this. I need you," she whispered.

His response was a hard thrust that shook him to the core, and as he went deeper inside of her, she moaned out her pleasure. "Yes!"

And then her body arched beneath him and he began moving inside of her, in and out, as her moans grew louder, more intense, more demanding and the eyes holding his looked at him with amazement and wonder. She began moving with him, their bodies in perfect rhythm.

Then she came again.

He felt the explosion of pleasure rip through her. Her fingers dug into his back and her legs locked around his waist, and he kept making love to her. Reality was better than any dream he could possibly have. He moved in and out of her, intensifying both their pleasure with every movement, feeling the urgency building up inside of her again.

Her next explosion triggered his and he screamed her name the exact moment she screamed his. He took her mouth in one final deep kiss, putting into it everything that he had, everything that was him. And moments later when the waves finally subsided, he was too weak, too satisfied, too far spent to move. But not wanting to crush her with his weight, he somehow managed to shift while keeping their bodies connected. He wasn't ready to sever the ties yet.

Feeling an aftermath of pleasure that he hadn't ever felt before, he buried his face in her breasts and wrapped his legs around her to lock her body in place with his, as they both closed their eyes in sheer exhaustion. The only word he could think of to describe what they had just shared was incredible.

As Chance's breathing began to slow, he knew that Kylie becoming a part of his life was a gift that he would cherish forever.

Chapter 12

Chance lay there and watched as Kylie awakened. Even before she fully opened her eyes, she covered her yawn, and it was then that he leaned over and gently pulled her hand away before capturing her mouth in his. Seconds later the same desire that was raging through him took over her. She sighed into his mouth and wrapped her arms around his neck, surrendering to the passion he evoked.

The mere memory of all the things they had done last night sent heat escalating through his body and making it harder not to take her again. The intensity of his love for her went well beyond the scope of his understanding, but as far as he was concerned it didn't really matter as long as he was smart enough to accept it. And he did.

He couldn't imagine ever being without her and while he'd watched her sleep, he had felt as if he couldn't breathe unless he had kissed her again. Now he was getting his fill, as he'd done last night while making love to her. They had made love more times than he could count, but he wasn't keeping numbers so it hadn't mattered. The important thing was that each time he'd open his arms she had come into them willingly, without any hesitation or reservation, and that had meant a lot to him.

When he slowly released her mouth he watched as she dragged in a shaky breath. It was pretty obvious that she had never been awakened in such a manner before. "Wow," she said softly. "What was that for?"

He smiled and brought her body closer to him. He wished he could tell her it was for being the woman he loved, but there was no way he could do that. At least not yet. "That was for being the special person you are, and for allowing me to spend so much time with you last night."

A crooked smile claimed her lips as she remembered. "Yes, we did spend a lot of time together, didn't we?" Even now the rock-solid feel of him pressed against her belly was making her hot and achy all over again.

His lips formed into a half grin. "Sweetheart, we did more than that. I spent so much time inside of you that a certain part of my body actually thinks that's where it belongs. It wants another visit and is worse than a junkie in need of a fix."

"Really?" she said, arching her back and automatically pressing her pelvis against his hard erection.

"Yeah, and if you keep that up—"

"What are you going to do?"

She gasped when he quickly took hold of her hips and lifted her leg to cross over his, locking their position. Before she could gather her next breath he shifted his body and entered her.

Once inside her warm depth, he began thrusting back and forth inside of her, while his hands, wrapped tightly around her waist, held her immobile. His mouth feasted on hers with the same intensity as the lower part of his body was taking her. Mating with her.

She reluctantly tore her mouth from his. "Wh-what about protection?" she asked barely able to get the words out.

He withdrew slowly and then sank back deep inside of her to the hilt. "I got it covered." And then he took her mouth again and her hips automatically bucked against his, reestablishing the rhythm they had created the night before.

After last night he should have been exhausted, but after sleeping with her nestled in his arms, his entire body was primed with more sexual energy than he'd ever had before. He could mate like this with her for hours. She was just that wet and he was just that needy.

She tore her mouth from his and dropped her head into his chest and moaned with each thrust he made into her body.

"Had enough?" he asked, refusing to stop or slow down. The sensations flowing through him were giving him added stamina, making him greedy.

She lifted her head and looked him in the eye. "No."

A single chuckle escaped him. "That's good," he said adjusting his angle. "Because I couldn't stop now even if you asked me to."

"What if I changed my mind and begged you to stop?"

"Forget it."

He started making little circles around her lips with his tongue. And then he began thrusting his tongue back and forth inside his mouth, mimicking the action going on below, using the same rhythm.

"Chance!"

He latched his gaze on her face, saw the intensity in her features and knew she was about ready to explode. "Let go, baby," he coaxed, knowing whenever she came he would, too.

She arched toward him, locked her body tighter to his. It was obvious from the way she was digging her fingers into his shoulders that he'd hit gold again and zeroed in on her G-spot, that sexually sensitive area that he had discovered last night had made her have multiple orgasms back-to-back, several times over.

He grabbed hold of her butt and slowed down his strokes, although it tortured him to do so. But he was attuned to her pleasure. He stroked slowly in and out of her, hitting her in that very special spot that made her moans become louder and her breath deeper. When she glanced down and saw the way he was moving in and out of her, she began mumbling. "Oh, yes, that's the spot. Go deeper, Chance. Please. Deeper."

He did what she asked and she surprised him when she began flexing her inner muscles, milking him for all it was worth. He began feeling sensuous contractions inch all through his groin. "Aw, hell."

He began stroking her with an intensity that almost bordered on obsession, intent on pushing her over the edge, the same way she was pushing him. She dropped her head back against his chest again and he was getting turned on even more from the way their bodies were vigorously mating.

"Had enough yet?" he asked, his voice ragged. He hoped she hadn't.

She lifted her face and shook her head. Her eyes, glazed with desire met his and she arched into him, letting him know her answer before she said the words. "Not enough. More."

"Be careful what you ask for, sweetheart," he said. "I'm a Steele, remember. I'm made to last."

And then he withdrew slowly, just long enough to adjust positions, and in a flash Kylie found herself on her back with her legs wrapped around the upper part of Chance's shoulders. And then he thrust inside of her to the hilt, harder and faster.

She screamed out his name, clung to him and succumbed to him as a rush of molten heat speared through her. When he screamed her name and pressed her hips she knew he had gotten caught up in the same exhilarating passion as she had.

She nipped at the corner of his lip and he leaned down and opened his mouth fully over hers, deepening the kiss to taste as much of her as he could. And at that moment, Kylie knew if another fifteen years went by without ever having taken part in something like this, she would survive because in a mere twelve hours Chance had given her enough lovemaking to last a lifetime.

"You have a beautiful home, Chance," she called out to him.

"Thanks," he answered from the bedroom.

Kylie stood leaning against the marble counter in Chance's kitchen. After enjoying their early morning delight, she had lain in bed, convinced that she couldn't move, and had wondered if she would ever be able to do so again. But he had gathered her into his arms like a newborn baby and had taken her into the bathroom to shower with him. It was a shower she doubted she would ever forget. She managed a smile and shook her head thinking that even now it was hard to believe that the woman who had made love to him beneath the spray of water had actually been her.

She had changed into her favorite capri pants after their shower, then she had fixed them a quick breakfast and he had talked her into going with him to the gym to watch him and his brothers play their regular

Saturday morning game of basketball. But first he needed to swing by his place to change clothes. Showing up on the courts wearing his tux would definitely give his brothers something to talk about for a long time.

On the drive over to his place he had told her that he'd had the house built a few years after his wife died, because he felt he could not get on with his life while still living in the home they'd shared together. Now here she was, waiting patiently while he changed into a T-shirt and jogging pants.

"Sure I can't get you anything?" he asked, coming into the kitchen and setting his gym bag on the counter beside her.

A smile touched her lips. "No thanks. You've given me too much already."

"You haven't seen or felt everything yet," he said, as he smoothed his hand over the bare skin of her arm before grabbing her curvy bottom to bring her closer to the fit of him. He dipped his head, kissing her still-swollen lips thoroughly.

"You know we can skip that game with my brothers," he murmured softly against her lips.

"Hmm, and deny them the chance to work off their competitive frustrations? I wouldn't dare," she said, grinning.

He gave her one of his most charming smiles. "Forget my brothers. I promise if we were to stay here I'd make it worth your while."

Her grin broadened. "There's no doubt in my mind that you would, but I'm not sure I can keep up with you, Chance."

He bent his head and nipped gently at her neck. "Hey, you've been doing a pretty good job so far."

Her laughter was low and husky. "Thanks, but I have only so much energy to spare. I may be younger than you but I'm definitely out of practice."

He took her hand, raised it to his lips and kissed her fingers. "If you're sure you're not ready to try the springs in my bed then I guess we'd better go."

While walking her out to the car, he said, "I've made reservations for us tonight at Cedar Keys."

She glanced up at him. "Cedar Keys?" She'd heard the place was rather expensive.

"Yes, Cedar Keys. My special lady deserves special treatment," he said, opening the car door for her.

My special lady. A part of Kylie wished that she was indeed his special lady and then immediately regretted the thought. Just because she was in love with him didn't mean he had to love her back. She had to remind herself that this weekend was about absolute pleasure. Love had nothing to do with it.

"Will your brothers wonder why I'm with you?"

Chance glanced over at her before starting the ignition. "They know we left the ball together last night, Kylie."

The insinuation of his statement gave her a moment's pause. "So chances are they know we spent the night together." It was a statement more so than a question.

"Not necessarily. For all they know I took you home and I went to my place after inviting you to join me this morning. But will it bother you if they've figured things out?"

"I know that it shouldn't," she said quietly. "But I am the mother of the girl their nephew has a crush on."

Chance lifted an eyebrow. "So?"

"So they might figure that I should be setting a better example."

Chance frowned. He reached over and took her hand in his. "Hey, we're spending time in Pleasure-land this weekend, remember? We don't have time to take any guilt trips. Besides, there's no need for one," he said gently. "One day you're going to have to accept that what we do is our business, Kylie. And we don't have to answer to anyone."

She drew in a long, unsteady breath. "I wish it was that easy for me to think that way, Chance. But after I got pregnant with Tiffany, my parents made sure that all their friends knew they had nothing to do with the way I turned out. I heard them call me a bad seed once. Since then I've tried so hard to be good and to raise Tiffany the right way."

He reached over and pulled her into his arms, hugging her close. "Oh, baby, you have. You're being too hard on yourself. No one is perfect, not even your parents. And they had no right to lay something that heavy on you. We all make mistakes. I bet if you were to clean out their closets you'll find something they'd rather leave hidden."

She shook her head. "I doubt it. You don't know my parents."

"Yes, I think I do. They aren't one of a kind, you know. There are others out there just like them."

A smile she couldn't contain curved her lips. "Yes, I know."

"Then remember that. Always keep that thought in mind."

He released her and Kylie thought she fell in love with him even more at that moment. "You're good at that, you know."

He glanced over at her as he began backing the car out the driveway. "Good at what?"

"Soothing my ruffled feathers."

He smiled. "Glad I could help."

"Hey, man, did you have to bring your own personal cheerleader?" Bas whispered as he set a screen for Chance to shoot.

Chance laughed as he made yet another shot and Kylie stood and cheered again. "Jealousy won't get you any points, Bas. You could have brought Cassandra."

Bas frowned. "Are you kidding? Can any of you imagine her sitting over there on the bleachers watching me get hot and sweaty?"

Donovan chuckled. "No, I don't think we can."

"Hey, will the three of you cut the crap and let's get some playtime?" Morgan growled, pushing Bas out of the way and getting the ball from Chance.

"Hey, that's a foul, Morgan," Chance called out, watching Morgan dribble the ball down the court to make a shot. He then turned to Bas. "What's his problem?"

"Seems like some lady he was interested in last night at the ball wasn't all that receptive," Bas said as they ran down the court to retrieve the stolen ball.

"Who?"

"The woman who could be Queen Latifah's twin, Helena Spears. He asked her out and she declined. She's probably the first woman who's ever turned down a dinner date with him. He evidently doesn't handle rejection well."

Chance grinned. "Evidently."

The game ended an hour or so later with Bas and Chance winning. Morgan, who'd made six fouls, would have gotten thrown out of the game had they been playing by real basketball rules.

Kylie sat patiently on the bleachers waiting for the men to come out of the locker room, where they had gone to shower and change. When Bas came out first, he crossed the gym to come over to talk to her.

"So," he asked dropping in the seat next to her, "what did you think of our game?"

She couldn't help but smile. "Interesting. A lot of rules were broken."

Bas chuckled. "Yeah, better broken rules than broken noses. We need this game every week to work off frustrations. Otherwise, we'd be at each other's throats at some point during the week."

"So I heard."

After a few moments of silence, Bas, who had a habit of shooting straight from the hip, said, "Chance has never brought a woman to watch us play before, so I figure you must be special."

Kylie gave him a wry glance. "Do you?"

"Yes, I do."

"That's good to know because I think he's special, too."

Bas shook his head and chuckled softly. "You don't seem too happy about it."

Kylie let out a sigh. "We should be concentrating on our kids."

"Hey, Marcus is a smart guy and from what I hear your Tiffany is a smart girl."

"Yes, but trouble has a way of finding even smart people."

"You're talking to someone who knows. Trouble used to be my middle name."

Kylie caught her bottom lip between her teeth. "Chance is a nice guy," she said quietly. "Marcus is lucky to have him for a father."

"That's the same thing Chance said about you."

Kylie glanced over at Bas. "What?"

"That you were a nice person and that Tiffany was lucky to have you as a mother." Bas then leaned forward. "Hey, do me a favor, will you?"

"And what favor is that?"

"You've made him happy and—"

"Me?"

"Yes, you. I've never seen him in such a good mood. Sometimes I think that smile is plastered to his face."

Kylie shook her head. "I have nothing to do with it."

"Yes, you do. At first he was all bent out of shape at the thought that Marcus's attention had gotten off his books and shifted to a girl, but once he met you then he saw why."

Kylie's eyebrows pulled together in a frown. "What do you mean?"

Bas smiled. "He was so taken with you that he could see how Marcus could be taken with Tiffany." When Kylie didn't say anything, Bas said, "Now getting back to that favor..."

"Yes?"

"Keep making Chance happy. He's had a lot of sadness in his life and if there's anyone who deserves to be happy, it's him. I think he's a pretty great guy."

Before Kylie could say anything, Bas stood, jumped off the bleachers to the court and called over his shoulder, "I'll go see what's keeping him."

Kylie leaned back and thought about what Bas had said. Before she could give it too much thought, every nerve ending in her body came instantly alive when Chance walked out of the locker room. He had changed into a pair of jeans and another T-shirt. He crossed the gym to her with a heart-stopping smile on his face.

Catching her breath, she decided to go down to meet him. As soon as she got close he leaned down and brushed his lips over hers. "Sorry for the delay. I had to talk to Morgan about something."

She nodded as he took her hand in his and led her out of the gym. "That's okay. I enjoyed chatting with Bas while I waited. Is Morgan okay? He was playing a mean game today. He committed a lot of fouls."

Chance's smile curved into a full grin. "Yes, they were intentional. He had a lot of frustrations to work off."

"Oh."

Snaking his arm around her waist, Chance snuggled her closer to his side as they walked to the car. "What were your plans for today?"

"I was going grocery shopping."

He laughed. "Hey, so was I. Do you want to go together?"

When Chance opened the car door and she slid inside, she glanced up at him and smiled. "Why not? It just might be fun."

Later that evening as Kylie finished getting dressed for dinner she thought that grocery shopping with Chance had not only been fun, it had been educational as well.

He had known what fruits were in season, he made sure she checked the expiration date on everything she purchased and he advised her to stay away from the generic brands, claiming there was a difference in taste.

And she had discovered that they liked the same foods, and the same flavor ice cream. In fact, they had almost argued about who would get the last half gallon of chocolate-chip cookie dough until one of the store clerks assured them there was a case in the back.

After their shopping adventure he had brought her home to unload her groceries and indicated he would return around seven to take her to dinner. It was almost seven now and she was ready.

Kylie smiled as she glanced at herself in the mirror. She was wearing a dress she had purchased earlier that year when she had attended her father's retirement party. Her mother had complimented her on how good she'd looked in it, and now she hoped Chance shared that same opinion. She was just about to add strawberry lip color to her lips when the phone rang. She quickly picked it up. "Hello."

"Hi, Mom."

"Tiffany! I'm glad you called. How's Disney World?"

"Disney World is fine but I think Gramma had too much of Mickey and Minnie for one day. Me and Gramps are going to leave her at the hotel and go to Epcot later. How was the ball last night?"

Kylie was surprised her daughter remembered anything about the ball. "It was nice. Your godmother's committee did an excellent job."

"Was Marcus's father there?"

Kylie raised an eyebrow, wondering why Tiffany wanted to know. "Yes, he was there."

"So you saw him?"

"Yes, I saw him."

"Was he with someone?"

Kylie refused to answer that. "Tiffany, why are you asking me questions about Marcus's father?"

"Oh, just curious. Marcus and I talked before I left and he's concerned that his dad doesn't date much."

"It's not the end of the world for a person not to date, Tiffany."

"I know and that's what I told Marcus since you don't date, either. Okay, Mom, I got to go, Gramps is waiting for me. Talk to you later."

"Okay, sweetheart, have fun and tell Mom and Dad hello."

After she hung up the phone Kylie decided to

cover all her bases in case Tiffany hit up her god-mother for answers about the ball. She quickly picked up the phone and dialed Lena's number. "Don't be surprised if you receive a call from Tiffany asking questions about last night's ball," she told her friend.

"What kind of questions?"

"Like who Chance was with."

Lena chuckled. "He was with you."

"Yes, but I prefer her not knowing that, Lena."

"Sure, if that's the way you want it."

"It is." Something in Lena's voice made Kylie wonder if her friend was all right and she decided to ask.

"No, not really. I met this gorgeous man last night at the ball. He asked me out and I turned him down."

"Why?"

"Kylie, you know the score. Do you know how many times I've been dropped, sometimes even before the first date, when the guy finds out Mom and I come as a pair."

"Not all guys will make a big deal out of it, Lena."

"Yes, but I'm tired of trying to figure out those who will and those who won't. I don't plan on dating for a while."

Kylie frowned. "I don't know if that's a good idea."

Lena chuckled. "Looks who's talking."

"My situation is different and you know it. I don't date because I prefer not to. You want to date but you're afraid to."

"I am not."

"You are, too."

"Okay, so maybe I am. What's wrong with me protecting myself against heartbreak?"

"You don't know that will happen for sure. And if a man doesn't want you because you care enough to see to your mother's welfare, then screw him."

"Umm, speaking of screw...where did you and Chance disappear to last night?"

Silence pulsed over the line for a brief second and then Kylie said, "He took me home."

"And?"

"And what?"

"And why do I think there's more to this story?"

"There is but I'd rather not discuss it now."

"Okay, just know that I'll be all ears at lunch on Wednesday."

"I doubt if you'll let me forget. Goodbye, and remember what to say if Tiffany calls asking questions."

As soon as Kylie hung up the phone she thought about her conversation with Lena. Lena was her very best friend, but there was no way Kylie would confess to her all she'd done with Chance last night and this morning. Just thinking about it made her feel mortified on one hand and giddy with pleasure on the other. Still, some things had to be kept from even your best friend. She could just imagine the look on Lena's face if she told her what had happened in the shower this morning, and how Chance had taken her against the wall while water sprayed down on them.

She glanced at the overnight bag on her bed. Chance had asked her to spend the night at his place and she'd agreed. Since this weekend was the only one they would share, she planned on making the most of it.

Chapter 13

"I hope you enjoyed tonight, Kylie."

She glanced up from studying the wine in her glass, locked gazes with Chance and smiled. "How could I not? Everything was wonderful. The food, the service, the location…my dinner date. Thanks for bringing me here, Chance."

A smile touched the corners of his lips. "I wanted our first real date to be special, somewhere that didn't serve hamburgers."

Kylie grinned. "And it was special." She was suddenly filled with regret knowing this had been their first real date and also their last. There was no way they could continue seeing each other after Marcus and Tiffany returned, but she didn't want to think about that now. They still had tonight and all day tomorrow.

"Do you want any dessert?" he asked, and she thought his voice had a kind of husky purr to it. The expression in his eyes wasn't helping matters any, either. She'd have dessert later, she thought. Chance wanted the same thing she wanted. A bed with both of them in it.

"None for me tonight, but thanks for asking. What about you? Do you have a sweet tooth?"

He shook his head and grinned. "No, not exactly. I think I'll pass, too."

He leaned over the table to make sure she was the only one who would hear his next words. "What I really want is to take you to my place, strip you naked and make love to you. All night long."

Only the flicker of her eyelids told him she had been shocked by such honesty. But then the heated look in her eyes told him how much she wanted what he wanted.

With self-control, she neatly folder her napkin and placed it on the table. Then she looked up and shot him a sexy grin. "Then I guess we should leave now, don't you?"

* * *

Kylie found herself glancing around Chance's home for the second time that day. She had given him her overnight bag and he had taken it to the bedroom.

He had surprised her. With the heated looks he'd been giving her all evening, she'd figured he would have pounced on her the first chance he got. She'd even expected him to pull the car to the side of the road like he'd done last night and kiss her senseless. If nothing else, she had fully expected him to strip her naked the moment she had stepped inside his home.

But he hadn't done any of those things and she thought he was controlling himself admirably. So much so that she was tempted to see just how far that control could go.

"Would you like a cup of coffee or anything?"

She turned when he reentered the room. He had removed his dinner jacket and tie, and now her gaze lingered on his white shirt as she thought about the chest it covered and remembered how she had smothered her face in that chest while he'd rocked back and forth inside her body, making her moan, groan and scream.

"No, I don't want any coffee. Thanks for asking. But there is something I want."

"What?"

"A kiss. It seems I've gotten addicted to them."

"Kisses?" he asked, slowly crossing the room to her.

"Yes, but only yours."

When he came to a stop in front of her, he reached out and wrapped his arms around her waist. In response, her arms wound around his neck. She raised her chin and looked him dead in the eyes and almost melted at the heat she saw there. When he leaned forward, she lifted her lips up for the kiss she knew she would get.

As soon as his mouth touched hers, she let out a deep, satisfied moan that she felt all the way to the pit of her stomach. And when he began stroking her tongue, with all the mastery that he possessed, she moaned some more. He tasted of the wine they'd had at dinner and of the peppermint he had popped into his mouth while walking her to the car. She enjoyed the flavor of both. When he deepened the kiss she forgot everything except for the way he was making her feel.

His arms were no longer around her waist. At some point in time they had moved and his hands were now cupping her bottom, pressing her closer to him, letting her feel the strength of his growing arousal.

He released her mouth long enough for her to draw in a breath. The same breath that hitched when his lips trailed to her throat and he branded her neck again.

"Chance," she whispered.

"Yes, sweetheart?"

She tilted her head back and met his gaze. "I thought you wanted to strip my clothes off."

"I do."

"What's stopping you?"

"You never said that I could."

Kylie stared at him, remembering that last night he had asked if it was okay to undress her. It seemed that Chance Steele operated with a code of honor and that endeared him to her even more. "All right, then, I'm giving you my permission."

He took a step back and she watched his gaze travel slowly over her body, from head to toe. When he looked up, his eyes lingered on the curves of her breasts visible in the low V-neckline. He realized she wasn't wearing a bra. She could tell by the look in his eyes. That same look made her nipples harden, become sensitive to the point where she could actually feel desire roll around in her stomach.

His gaze then moved to the hemline of her dress. It was longer than the one she'd worn last night, but he seemed mesmerized by the front split, probably wondering what she had or didn't have on underneath.

"Last night I thought you looked simply gorgeous in black. But tonight I think you look sexy as hell in red," he said in a husky voice.

She blinked when she watched him back up a few steps and then walk over to the sofa and sat down. "Come here, Kylie," he said in a voice that sounded strained even to her ears.

She stared at him, confused. How was he going to strip her bare while sitting down?

"Kylie?"

Deciding she would soon find out, she crossed the room to him.

"Lift your leg in my lap so I can take off your shoes."

She did what he asked and he took off her shoes one at a time. When she was about ready to place her foot back on the floor, he kept it in his lap, resting against his hard erection while he slid his hand up her leg a little farther, going underneath her dress to touch the center of her thighs, only to discover her panty hose was a barrier.

Apparently deciding a pair of Hanes wouldn't stop him from doing what he wanted, he placed her foot on the floor then eased to the edge of the sofa and reached both hands under her dress to work the panty hose down her hips. She stepped out of them and then kicked them aside.

"Now put your right leg back in my lap."

Again she did as he requested and this time he was able to slide his hand a little farther up her leg than before. She moaned out loud when his finger touched her center and slowly stroked her.

"Ahh, just as I thought," he leaned in closer to say. "You aren't wearing any panties."

His words hardly registered. All she could think about was the feel of his fingers inside of her, making her even wetter.

"Let me see just what else you aren't wearing tonight, Kylie."

Before she could gather her next breath, he reached up with his free hand and yanked the top part of her dress down. Her breasts spilled free right in his face.

"Place your hands on my shoulders, bend your knee a little more and lean toward me."

The moment she did so, he captured a breast in his mouth and his tongue stroked it, just like his fingers were stroking her.

She clutched at his shoulders, unable to hold back just how his mouth and fingers were making her feel. Chance definitely knew how to work both ends at the same time. She was melting from the inside out. If he continued doing this for much longer she doubted even his shoulders would be able to support her.

He let go of her breast and leaned forward. "Are you ready for me, Kylie?" he whispered hotly in her ear.

Unable to answer, she nodded.

"That's good because I've been ready for you all day. And tonight at dinner it was hard for me not to spread you out on the table and make you the only entrée I wanted to feast on."

At his words an all-consuming need raced through her body and she cried out his name when she felt the first sign of an explosion on the horizon. "Chance, I need you."

"And where do you need me, baby?"

"Inside of me," she whispered.

He suddenly lifted her in strong arms, and she closed her eyes and pressed her face against his chest.

Her eyes opened when she felt herself being placed on a hard, solid surface. He had sat her on his kitchen counter. "Chance?"

He smiled as he began taking off his shirt and removing his pants. "When I saw you in here today, standing in this very spot, I knew I had to do this. I want to take you right here. Right now," he said, quickly putting on a condom.

"Here? Now? Are you serious?"

"Oh, yes."

He then pulled her dress over her head and tossed it to the floor to join his own discarded clothing. Before she could say another word, or let out another breath, he took hold of her hips, opened her thighs and guided his shaft inside of her.

And then the thrusting began. She wrapped her arms around his neck as delicious sensations began engulfing her. "This is insane," she said, leaning forward and nipping the corner of his mouth.

"No," he said in a husky voice as his body continued to mate with hers. "This is a dream come true. A fantasy in the making. So enjoy."

And she did. He drew her closer and she spread her legs wider to accommodate him. He kissed her deeply. Then he released her mouth to pay homage to her breasts again, flicking his tongue across each nipple, sucking one and then the other, causing a sensuous tension to coil deep within her womb.

"Chance!"

The explosion hit and she cried out, dug her fingers deep in his shoulders as sensation after sensation engulfed her. She thought she would die then and there from consuming so much pleasure.

And then she felt his body jerk and knew he was experiencing one hell of an orgasm as well. She reached out and held him as he shuddered uncontrollably with his release.

It was awhile before either could catch their breaths, and when they did, neither seemed inclined to move. So she inched closer, and with as much strength as she could muster, she tightened her legs around him, enjoying the feel of him still buried inside of her. When he was finally able to lift his head to meet her eyes, she gave him a sated smile. "I've heard that things can get pretty hot in a kitchen, but this is a bit much, don't you think?" she whispered with barely enough breath.

He reached out and caressed her cheek. "And this isn't as hot as it will get for us."

That bit of news made her inch even closer to him. "It's not?"

"No, it's not. You haven't seen or experienced anything yet."

Kylie wondered what else there was. They had made love in a bed, in the shower, on the kitchen counter...

"You ever do it in a hot tub?"

His question got her immediate attention. "No."

He smiled. "Good. Then this ought to be fun."

Late Sunday afternoon after returning home, Kylie stood in front of her bedroom mirror and gazed at her reflection. With her messed up hair, kiss-swollen lips and hickeys on both sides of her neck, she definitely looked like a woman who had let go and indulged in her sensuous side. Naughty was too mild a word to describe how she had acted this weekend. Wanton and loose were probably better.

"Hey, what are you doing? Looking for a spot that I missed?" Chance asked, entering the room. He walked up behind her, wrapped his arms around her and settled her body back against his.

Kylie thought him missing a spot was impossible. It had started out very innocent with them enjoying a bowl of ice cream after lunch. Then for no reason at all he had squirted caramel topping all over her, and moments later began licking every inch of her skin to get it off. And she had reciprocated, squirted him and licked every inch of him. She had to admit that for once in her life she had thrown caution to the wind and yielded to temptation.

"What are you thinking about, sweetheart?"

She met his gaze in the mirror and leaned back against him when he tightened his arms around her. "You. Me. And what a wonderful weekend we had. I wish it didn't have to end."

"It doesn't."

She shook her head and grinned. "Yes, it does. Have you forgotten the kids will be back tomorrow?"

"No, I didn't forget but that shouldn't have any bearing on us."

She turned around to face him. "Of course it does. Surely you don't expect us to still swap beds with the kids around?"

He frowned. "No, but I do expect us to continue to see each other. And if we have to be discreet whenever we do share a bed, then we will."

"And what about the kids?"

"Tomorrow we can tell them that we've decided to start seeing each other."

She took a step back. "No, I don't think that's a good idea."

Chance rubbed his hand down his face. "Don't tell me we're back to that again."

"As far as I'm concerned we never left it."

"Then what was this weekend about, Kylie?"

"It was about us indulging in our fantasies. But now it's time to return to the real world, Chance, and there's no way I can let Tiffany know that I was involved in a weekend affair with you."

Angrily, he reached out and gripped her shoulders. "A weekend affair? That's all this was to you?"

She yanked away from him. "Why? Was it supposed to be something else?"

"I had hoped so," he said quietly, trying to get his anger and frustrations under control. "The start of a committed relationship was how I saw things."

"But I can't become involved with anyone until Tiffany leaves home."

"Why?"

"Because I can't!"

"Then let me tell you what I think is your reason, which in my opinion is a damn poor excuse. Your parents have convinced you that getting pregnant at sixteen was a bad thing, and every since then you have worked your ass off trying to be a good girl in their eyes. So much so that you won't allow a man in your life. At first I thought it was all about the men in your life letting you down and not being dependable, and that still may be a part of it. But since you claim you trust me, why are you so afraid of letting me into your life?"

"I have to set an example for my daughter. Why can't you understand that?"

He frowned. "And not having a real life, not having a man around to show her how two people can share a loving relationship is setting an example for her?"

"There's more to life than people getting involved, Chance."

"What about people falling in love? Would it mean anything if I were to tell you that I love you? That I fell in love with you probably the first time I saw you that day?"

Kylie's eyes widened and then she shook her head and felt the tears that stung her eyes. "No, it wouldn't matter because I could tell you the same thing, Chance. I love you, too. And I probably fell in love with you that day as well."

"But then—"

"No. You loving me and me loving you won't make it okay. We still have to put our kids first. They think they're in love, too, and we can't downplay their feelings just because we've discovered ours. Just think of how it will look. The father loves the mother and the daughter loves the son. How dysfunctional can that be?"

His frown deepened. "So what are you suggesting? That we wait to see what becomes of our kids' romance before seeking our own? Well, I don't plan to do that. If you love me, and I mean truly love me, you'll know that we'll work things out together. But you have to be willing to step out on love and believe it."

She bowed her head and took a deep breath and then she looked back at him. "No, it won't work, Chance. Please try to understand. There are times in life when sacrifices have to be made."

"Well, if you're willing to let your love for me be the sacrificial lamb then it must not be the real thing, Kylie, because I can't think of anything that will ever stop me from loving you and wanting a committed relationship with you."

Without saying anything else he walked out of the room, and moments later Kylie heard the door slam shut behind him.

Chapter 14

"Mom?"

"Hmm?"

"Are you sure you're okay?"

Kylie pulled two bottles of apple juice out of the refrigerator before turning to her daughter. "I'm okay, sweetheart. What makes you think I'm not?"

Tiffany lifted one shoulder in a dainty shrug. "I don't know. It's just a feeling I have. Every since you picked me up from the airport yesterday you've been quiet."

"Well, I guess I have a lot on my mind, but I'm okay."

"Why are you still wearing that scarf? You usually don't wear scarfs."

Kylie's hand automatically went to the scarf around her neck, the one she was wearing to hide the two hickeys that Chance had placed there. "My throat had gotten sort of scratchy with the changing of the weather, I guess. I thought I'd take all precautions. The last thing I need to catch is a cold."

"But you're wearing it in the house."

Kylie gave Tiffany a pointed look. "I'm aware of where I am Tiffany. Is wearing a scarf in the house a crime?"

"No, ma'am."

"Okay, then."

The kitchen got silent and Kylie regretted having gotten upset with Tiffany when she was only showing her concern. With a mantle of guilt on her shoulders, Kylie crossed the room and sat down at the table opposite her daughter. "Hey, how about you and I going to a movie this weekend?" she asked, trying to reclaim the easy camaraderie they'd started recently, at least before this past weekend.

Tiffany smiled. "Oh, that'll be neat. Will it be okay to invite Marcus and his dad?"

Kylie's body tensed with her daughter's question. The last person she wanted to be around this weekend was Chance. "I was hoping we could make it a girls' thing. We could even invite Lena to come with us."

"That sounds like fun, Mom, but I was hoping I could get to see Marcus this weekend."

"Didn't you see him at school today?"

"Yes."

"And won't you see him again tomorrow?"

"Yes."

"And the next day and the day after?"

"Yes, Mom, but you and Mr. Steele promised that we could have supervised outings and it's been almost three weeks since we went camping."

Kylie sighed. A part of her regretted having made that promise but at the time both she and Chance had known it was the best thing to keep the budding romance between their offspring under control. "Okay, then I'll take the both of you. There's no need to bother Chance this weekend and—"

"Mom, if you take us, it'll seem as if you're babysitting us. If both you and Mr. Steele go then it will be a foursome and it won't be so obvious that you're there to spy on us."

Kylie rolled her eyes. "I'd be there as a chaperone, Tiffany."

"Same difference."

Not wanting to get into an argument with her daughter, Kylie stood and said, "Have Marcus check to see if his father is free this weekend. Chance is a busy man and might have made other plans."

Later that night Kylie lay in bed and every so often she would glance over at the phone. Chance had made it a habit to call her around this time every night, but she knew after Sunday chances were that he wouldn't be calling any time soon, if ever. And a part of her thought maybe it was for the best. He thought he had all the answers, but he would never understand the guilt trip her parents had placed on her shoulders after she'd gotten pregnant.

As she cuddled under the covers she thought about the weekend she had spent with Chance. There was no denying that it had been a fantasy come true, and heat flooded through her just thinking about all they had done. In fact today at the florist when she'd been alone her body actually trembled with the memories that were so vivid in her mind.

Their first date had been everything a first date should be, and what he probably hadn't even realized was, although it had been their first date, it had been her *first* date period. She and Sam had been too young to actually date and she hadn't gone out to dinner with any other man. So in reality, Chance had been her first in a lot of ways.

Tears blurring her eyes, she glanced over at the phone. She might as well get used to him not calling her ever again.

Chance threw onto his desk the document he'd been reading and glanced at the clock. Not that he was counting, but it had been three days, sixteen hours and forty-five minutes since he had last seen and talked to Kylie.

After what she had said to him on Sunday evening, she should have been the last person on his mind. She had decided that love or no love, there would not be a future for them.

Chance leaned back in his chair and hooked his hands behind his head. Dammit, he didn't want that. He wanted a life with her, a life that included marriage. Kylie was being more than stubborn. She was being downright difficult.

He couldn't help but remember their weekend together, and the days and nights they had shared. Those memories would sustain him in the coming months. He would need them.

He walked over to the window and stared out at Charlotte's skyline. It was almost two in the afternoon. Kylie would be at her shop. Was she thinking about him the way he was thinking about her? Probably not.

But she had admitted that she loved him.

He should have known that when a woman gave herself as completely to a man as Kylie had done to him this past weekend that love was involved. One thing was for certain: there was still Marcus and Tiffany to deal with, and because of their kids, Kylie couldn't put distance between them regardless of how much she might want to.

Whether she liked it or not, she hadn't seen the last of him.

"I don't know what, but something happened this weekend between our parents, Marcus," Tiffany whispered.

Marcus, who was sitting across from her in the library, glanced around to make sure Mrs. Kennard, the librarian who had a strict no-talking policy, wasn't anywhere close by. "Yes, I know," he whispered back. "This weekend was supposed to get them to together, not pull them apart. What do you think happened?"

Tiffany shook her head. "I don't know but I do know they spent time together this weekend."

Marcus lifted a brow. "And how do you know that?"

"Because Carly Owens said she saw them together at the grocery store."

"The grocery store? What were they doing at the grocery store?"

"Carly said they were actually shopping together. They didn't see her but she saw them. She said my mom had her cart and your dad had his, but they had come together in the same car."

"And she's sure it was *our* parents?"

"Yes, she's sure. She's met the both of them before but at different times."

"Umm, I find that interesting. If they were friendly enough to go grocery shopping together then what happened?"

Tiffany sighed. "I don't know. And there's also something else." She leaned in closer to make sure the students sitting at the other table didn't hear her. "My mom had a hickey on her neck and I think your dad put it there."

Disbelief flickered in Marcus's eyes. "You're kidding."

"No. She's been wearing a scarf to hide it, but I saw it anyway when she took the scarf off thinking I wasn't around."

Marcus nodded. "That means they had to have kissed."

"Right."

"Then what happened to make them start acting funny?"

Tiffany shook her head. "Who knows? Adults can be weird that way. Did your dad say that he would be available to go to the movies with us on Saturday?" Tiffany asked.

"I haven't asked him yet. He hasn't been in the best of moods since I got back."

"Neither has my mom. If after this weekend at the movies they're still not getting along, then we have to do something. I know they really like each other, but now I'm worried because your dad hasn't been calling at night like he used to do. I've been checking the caller ID every morning but your phone number isn't showing up."

"So what do you think we should do?"

Tiffany scrunched her forehead and then moments later a smile touched her features. "I have an idea but we may have to get an adult to help us pull it off."

Marcus glanced around again for Mrs. Kennard, and then turned back to Tiffany. "An adult like who?"

Tiffany thought about her godmother and

decided it wouldn't be a good idea to solicit her help. "How about one of your uncles? The one you said who likes to have fun."

Marcus sighed. "That's Uncle Donovan, and this sounds serious."

"It is. We'll see how things go with them this weekend, but if they still aren't on the best of terms, we go to Plan B."

"What's Plan B?" Marcus asked.

Tiffany leaned in closer. "Here it is, so listen up."

Kylie chewed the corner of her lip as she watched Chance and Marcus get out of the SUV and begin walking toward her front door. That deep fluttering in her heart and the sensations that rolled around in her stomach whenever she saw Chance made her release the breath she'd been holding. She could only stand at the window and stare out at him, providing irrefutable proof of just how much she had missed seeing him these past few days, missed talking with him…making love with him.

A part of her questioned the sanity in not giving in to the love she felt for him. Even Lena had raked her over the coals during their lunch meeting that week when she'd told her best friend that Chance had admitted his love and she had admitted hers.

Lena staunchly refused to agree with Kylie that this was one of those no-win situations where love wasn't enough.

"Mom, are Marcus and Mr. Steele here?"

Kylie turned away from the window upon hearing the excitement in her daughter's voice. "Yes, they just arrived."

"Good. I'll go open the door for them." And then Tiffany raced off.

A few moments later Kylie could hear the deep sexiness of Chance's voice all the way from the foyer, and the sound sent sizzling heat all through her body. Taking a deep breath, she grabbed her coat off the back of the sofa and left the living room to join everyone in the foyer.

The moment she rounded the corner she felt Chance's gaze on her. And the moment her eyes locked with his dark brown ones, she almost forgot to breathe. For some reason she couldn't look away.

"Hi, Kylie."

"Chance."

"You look nice."

"Thanks." Kylie inwardly sighed. Holding a conversation with him used to be so easy and now she was finding it too hard.

"Hi, Ms. Hagan."

Her gaze moved from Chance to Marcus and for a second she thought she saw a worried glint in his eyes. She smiled affectionately. "Hello, Marcus. How was your trip to Busch Gardens?"

"It was fun. I was telling Tiffany about it. Maybe the four of us could go there this summer."

Kylie nodded, although she doubted it.

"Is everyone ready to go?" Chance asked. "We don't want to be late for the movie."

Marcus and Tiffany rushed out the door leaving their parents alone in the foyer. Chance turned to her. "I meant what I said earlier, Kylie. You look nice in that pantsuit. That color looks good on you. But I think any color looks good on you."

"Thanks." She had decided to wear a lime-green linen pantsuit and instead of pinning her braids up she let them tumble about her shoulders.

She stared at the floor for a second and then glanced back up at him. "You look nice, too." She decided not to tell him that she'd always thought he looked suave in a suit, but sexy as hell in a pair of jeans.

"Thanks. Are you ready to go?"

"Yes."

"And, Kylie, no matter what's going on with us, let's make sure the kids have a good time tonight, all right?"

"All right."

They then walked out the door to join their kids in the SUV.

They saw the new Harry Potter movie.

Kylie was certain it had been a good movie but she hadn't fully concentrated on what was happening on the big screen. Instead her concentration had been on the man who had sat next to her. They had barely exchanged a single word but all during the movie she could feel the weight of his heavy stare. More than once she had glanced his way in the semi-darkened theater to find him watching her.

Too often she had been tempted to reach out and slip her hand in his, filled with an intense desire to touch him, to feel his heat. It didn't take much for her to remember that heat, how he had consumed her with it whenever he touched her, kissed her or made love to her.

"Wasn't the movie awesome, Mom?" Tiffany said with enthusiasm in her voice as they left the theater and walked through the parking lot back to Chance's truck.

"Yes, it was nice."

Then Marcus and Tiffany got into conversations about all their favorite scenes and left Kylie and

Chance to do nothing but remain silent. He didn't seem inclined to make idle chatter and neither did she. He opened the truck door for her and when their hands brushed she felt him tense the exact moment she did.

"Can we stop for ice cream?" Tiffany asked when everyone was inside the truck and buckled up.

"No," Kylie and Chance called out simultaneously, and then glanced over at each other. Chance cleared his throat and said in a more subdued voice. "I'm going out of town on Monday and there's a lot I need to do to get prepared for the trip."

"And I need to look over my accounting books tonight," Kylie added.

Both Chance and Kylie heard the disappointment in Tiffany's and Marcus's voices but decided that a movie had been enough. There was no way they could sit across from each other and eat ice cream without remembering what had happened the last time they'd done so. It had been the cause of their "lick me all over" party.

All it took was a memory—of Chance stripping her naked in her kitchen, licking sticky caramel sauce off her body—and Kylie's palms started to tingle. Her breasts suddenly felt heavy, her nipples tight, and erotic sensations built up inside of her, settling right smack between her legs. She forced a deep breath of air into her lungs thinking that this was definitely not the time nor the place for arousal.

She glanced over at Chance, and as if he felt her gaze on him, he turned to her. From the heated look in his eyes she could tell he too was remembering what they'd done that Sunday afternoon in her kitchen.

Kylie settled back in her seat. This was going to be one long and extremely hot ride home.

It was time for Plan B.

Marcus and Tiffany wasted no time putting it into action. On Tuesday they had Donovan Steele's full attention as they filled him in on the failure of Plan A. "So as you can see, Uncle Donovan, we need your help."

Donovan leaned back and looked at the both of them. Marcus had contacted him on his cell phone asking that he meet them after school on the football bleachers.

Donovan shook his head. "Let me get this straight. The two of you aren't girlfriend and boyfriend? You aren't madly in love? And you only pretended you were to get your parents together?" he asked incredulously.

Both Tiffany and Marcus nodded. "That's right,"

Marcus said. "Tiffany and I are best friends and we thought it was a good plan. Things were going along smoothly but something happened that weekend the two of us left town."

Donovan lifted a brow. "And what do you think happened?"

"We don't know but before we left they were beginning to like each other a lot, but now we're not sure how they feel."

Donovan had heard the story from Bas and Morgan but he wasn't about to share the information with these two. "So what do you need for me to do?"

"Help us," Tiffany said.

Donovan was confused. "Help you do what?"

It was Marcus who answered. "Carry out our plan to get our parents together."

Donovan crossed his arms over his chest, not believing what they were asking of him. He loved his nephew but was he willing to incur his oldest brother's wrath? "I think you had better tell me about this plan first."

Marcus nodded. "I'll let Tiffany explain things since it's her idea. But I think it's a good one."

Donovan doubted it was all that good but decided to listen anyway. Twenty minutes later a smile touched his lips. He hated to admit it but he liked their idea, although it could use a little tweaking here and there to make sure neither Chance nor Kylie panicked and got the police involved. There was no doubt that Chance would be mad in the beginning, but in the end odds were he would be a very happy man. "Okay, count me in. I'll help but only on one condition."

"What?" Marcus asked.

"That you modify your plan somewhat."

Marcus and Tiffany quickly agreed.

Donovan then smiled and said, "Now, I think that this is the way we should handle things...."

Chapter 15

Late Friday night Kylie glanced over at the clock on her nightstand the moment the telephone rang. It was almost midnight. She suddenly got a funny feeling in her stomach. Was it Chance? The last time she had seen him was Sunday night when they had all gone to the movies.

Deciding that answering was the only way to determine who her caller was, she reached out and picked up the phone. "Hello?"

"Mom?"

Kylie shot straight up in bed. The voice sounded

like Tiffany's, but there was no way her daughter could be calling her when she was down the hall in her bed sleeping.

"Mom? Are you there? It's me."

Kylie jumped out of bed to her feet. "Tiffany! Where are you?"

"Mom, I'm fine."

Kylie angrily began pacing her bedroom. "Fine, nothing! Where are you, young lady? No one gave you permission to leave this house. How dare you pull something like that!"

"Mom, please calm down. I'm fine. Marcus and I are together."

"What?" Kylie screamed at the top of her lungs, before collapsing in the wingback chair in her room. "What do you mean you and Marcus are together? It's after midnight. No one gave you permission to—"

"Mom, Marcus and I have been thinking."

Kylie gripped the phone tightly in her hand. "Thinking? The two of you have been thinking? Fine, then think at your own houses. I want you home immediately!"

"Not until you and Mr. Steele promise to become friends again."

Kylie frowned. What was Tiffany talking about?

"Listen, honey, Chance and I are friends. You need to come home."

"The two of you didn't act like it Sunday night. You barely said two words to each other. If Mr. Steele is going to be our in-law one day, then the two of you are going to have to get along."

Kylie threw her head back and began silently counting to ten, not believing the conversation she and her daughter were having. "Look, Tiffany, I don't know where you are but I want you to end this call right now and come home. Better yet, tell me where you are and I'll come and get you."

"No, Mom, I can't do that. Marcus and I aren't going to do anything we shouldn't, so don't worry about that."

"But I am worried about that! You're only fifteen, it's after midnight and you're out somewhere with a boy when you should be home sleeping in your bed. How dare you tell me not to worry!"

"Then maybe I should ask you to trust me, and to also trust Marcus. We're in a safe location and we won't do anything that you and Mr. Steele will be ashamed of."

"That's not the point!"

"It is the point, Mom. You and Mr. Steele are going to have to trust us. Marcus and I figured the reason the two of you can't get along is because you don't trust each other and you don't trust us."

Kylie struggled to keep her voice calm. "I do trust Chance and I've tried to stop being so uptight and to start trusting you more, but I see doing so was a mistake. You either come home within the next thirty minutes or I'm calling the police."

"Mom, please don't. All it will do is cause unnecessary embarrassment for me and Marcus."

"Tough! The two of you should have thought of that sooner."

"Mom, I'm serious. If you call the police then we won't come back. All we need is time to talk."

"And just what do the two of you have to talk about that you had to sneak out in the middle of the night to do it?"

"We need to talk about you and Mr. Steele and your inability to get along."

"We can get along!"

"Then you sure fooled us. You *were* getting along, then something happened. We don't know what but the two of you sure acted like you were avoiding each other on Sunday."

"Tiffany, I—"

"Good night, Mom. We'll call you in the morning and tell you our decision."

Kylie's stomach dropped to the floor. "Your decision about what?"

"About whatever we decide. Marcus has to call his father now. Goodbye, Mom. I'll talk to you in the morning, and I promise Marcus and I won't do anything."

Before Kylie could open her mouth to say another word, there was a resounding click in her ear.

Kylie quickly snatched up the phone the moment it rang again five minutes later knowing it was Chance.

"Kylie, you okay?"

His deep, husky voice had a comforting effect on her. "Oh, Chance, what are we going to do?"

"You didn't call the police, did you?"

"No."

"Good. I got a chance to talk to the both of them and—"

"Can you believe what they've done? Just wait until I see them. I'm going to—"

"Calm down, Kylie."

"Calm down? My child is out somewhere after midnight and you want me to calm down?"

"Yes. My child is out there, too. One good thing is that they're together."

"You think that's a good thing?"

"I trust Marcus, Kylie. He won't let anything happen to Tiffany. And he gave me his word that they won't do anything they aren't supposed to do."

Kylie glanced out her bedroom window. A fist tightened around her heart knowing her little girl was out there somewhere. "Yes, that's the same thing Tiffany said," she murmured quietly. "And you're right, we're going to have to trust them."

Kylie was quiet for a long while, then she said, "Did Marcus tell you why they did it?"

"Yes, he told me."

"I thought we acted pretty normal on Sunday night," she said.

"Yeah, but I guess they still picked up on something."

"Well, even if they thought we weren't on the best of terms, it wasn't any of their business!"

"Oh? You finally agree with me about that?"

Kylie frowned. "I'm serious, Chance."

"I've always been serious about that." He then asked, "Where are you now?"

"In my bedroom."

"How about going downstairs and putting some coffee on. I doubt if either of us will get much sleep tonight and if we're going to worry, we might as well do it together. I'm on my way over."

"All right. I'll have the coffee ready when you get here."

Chance made it to Kylie's house in less than ten minutes. She met him at the door with a cup of steaming hot coffee.

As if it was the most natural thing to do, he leaned over and kissed her lips. "You okay?" he asked quietly, after taking the cup from her hand and following her into her living room, where he sat down on the leather sofa beside her.

"Yes, I'm okay. But I'm still worried about them, Chance. I didn't think to ask how they were getting around. I assumed Marcus took his car."

Chance nodded after taking a sip of his coffee. "Yes, he has it. Boy, he's going to be grounded for life."

"So is Tiffany and she hasn't started driving yet. And just to think I had considered surprising her with a car for her sixteenth birthday. She might as well kiss that surprise goodbye."

"And they pulled this just to make a statement that they didn't like the way we acted on Sunday. If that doesn't beat all," Chance said.

"Yeah, I guess it means a lot to them for us to get along."

"But it's not like we argued or anything, Kylie."

She inhaled deeply. "I know but I guess they were watching us more closely then we thought. You have to admit we were rather distant to each other."

"Yes, we were," he readily admitted it. "And I didn't like it."

She met his gaze and said, "Neither did I."

After a few moments of silence she added, "Do you think we're doing the right thing by not calling the police?"

"Yes. But I did contact my brothers. There was no way I could not let them know. At least I was able to reach Bas and Morgan. Evidently Donovan is still somewhere out on the town and he isn't answering his cell. But I'll talk to him tomorrow. And I notified my cousins, as well, in case Marcus contacts them."

Kylie's nodded. "I forgot about your basketball game in the morning."

Chance shook his head. "Yeah, but there's no way I'm going to go anyplace until the kids come home."

"They will come home, won't they, Chance?"

When he heard the trembling in her voice, he set his cup on the table and wrapped his arms around her shoulders. It felt good to hold her again. "Yes, they'll come home. When they get hungry, they'll be back."

His words made Kylie smile. "Yeah, Tiffany definitely likes to eat."

"And so does Marcus."

Kylie cuddled deeper into Chance's warm embrace. It felt good to be held by a man who cared about her. A man who'd told her he loved her. A man she knew she could depend on. "Where do you think they'll sleep tonight?"

Chance shrugged. "Either in the car or at a hotel."

Kylie pulled back and looked at Chance. "Are they old enough to get a hotel room on their own?"

"It depends on where they go. To some hotel owners, money and not age is the determining factor."

Kylie really hadn't wanted to hear that. More than anything she had to remember that Tiffany said she and Marcus wouldn't do anything. She had promised.

"Come here and lay beside me. You must be tired."

She automatically did what he suggested without thinking twice about it. He stretched out his legs on the sofa to accommodate her and gently held her as they lay side by side. Before he had arrived, she had changed out of her nightgown into a pair of silk lounging pants and top. Heat curled through her when he wrapped his arms around her. It felt good knowing she wasn't alone now.

"Try to get some sleep."

"I don't think I can, Chance. I want my baby home." A few moments later, sleepily she said, "Did I ever tell you about the first time I let Tiffany sleep somewhere other than her own bed?"

"No, I don't think that you did."

"She was two and my parents had finally acknowledged that they had a grandchild and wanted some bonding time. At first I wasn't going to let her go but then Lena convinced me that I should. I barely slept that entire night knowing she wasn't in the house. I finally was able to sleep only after going into her room and stretching out on the floor beside her little bed. Now isn't that pathetic?"

"No, it sounds to me like you were a mother who had missed her child and needed the connection." After a few moments he added, "It works like that for adults, too, you know."

She lifted her head and met his gaze. "Does it?"

"Yes." He reached out and stroked her cheek with one finger. "You slept in my bed that one night but that's all it took for me to get used to your presence. All this week I found myself reaching out, as if you were still there, wanting that connection."

Kylie's stomach knotted when her gaze slipped to his mouth and she remembered how that mouth had driven her crazy in so many different ways. She remembered the taste of it, the feel of it. She also remembered something else. The amount of love she had in her heart for this one particular man.

"Oh, Chance." She reached up and tightened her arms around his neck at the same time she leaned up for his kiss.

With agonizing slowness he took her mouth, claimed it, branded it. His tongue made love to her mouth. The more it did, the more she became fully aware of the steady, strong arms holding her. They were protective arms. They were arms that would shield her from any storm, whether raging or mild. They were arms that would always be there to hold her when she needed to be held. It had been late in coming but she realized that now.

Moments later when he lifted his mouth she let out a satisfied sigh. "Thanks. I needed that."

He looked at her and smiled. "So did I."

Determined to maintain control of the situation he then said, "Now let's try to get some rest so we can be well-rested to give our kids hell when they come back home."

"Yes, *our* kids." Kylie said the words as if they suddenly had new meaning to her.

As he pulled her closer she settled against his comforting muscular form and believed that from this time forward somehow everything was going to be all right.

"Mom?"

"Dad?"

Chance slowly opened his eyes. Had he been dreaming or had he actually heard Tiffany's and Marcus's voices? The first thing he noticed was that he was stretched out on the sofa with Kylie lying beside him, her head resting on his chest. That would not have been so bad if his hand wasn't possessively cupping her bottom or one of her legs wasn't entwined with his. Even her hand was resting pretty darn close to the fly on his jeans.

He sucked in a deep breath, letting the scent of her fill his nostrils. She was still asleep, but he could remember a time that weekend when he had patiently waited for her to wake up so that he could—

"Dad?"

"Mom?"

Chance swallowed as he slowly glanced across

the room and his gaze lit on two pairs of curious eyes. He blinked. No, make that three.

He quickly sat up and the movement startled Kylie out of a sound sleep. "Chance, what's wrong?" she asked sluggishly, slowly coming awake.

He shifted his gaze from the three sets of eyes to her still-drowsy ones. "Wake up, sweetheart, the kids are back," he whispered.

She blinked. "What?"

"The kids are home."

She was off the sofa in a flash. He had to catch her to keep her from stumbling. "Tiffany! Marcus! We've been so worried about you," she said hugging them so tight Chance wondered how they were able to breathe.

Then as if it finally hit her what they had done, she stepped back, placed her hands on her hips and gave them one hell of a fierce frown. "The two of you have a lot of explaining to do."

"Seems they aren't the only ones," Donovan Steele said in a low voice, after clearing his throat.

Kylie jumped and jerked her head around. She hadn't seen Chance's youngest brother standing at the edge of the foyer. "Where did you find them?" she asked, tossing her mussed-up braids over her shoulders.

Before Donovan could answer, Tiffany said, "He didn't find us. We were with him the entire time. We spent the night over at his house."

"What?" That loud exclamation came from both Kylie and Chance at the same time.

"And we had so much fun," Marcus said, smiling. "The three of us played video games until—"

"What the hell do you mean you were with him the entire time?" Chance shouted, coming to his feet beside Kylie.

"Dad, don't get mad at Uncle Donovan," Marcus said, rushing in. "I can explain."

Donovan smiled as he leaned against the wall. "Yes, Chance, let him explain. And trust me, it's a doozy. And I think you and Kylie might want to be sitting down when you hear it."

Chapter 16

"Let me make sure I have this right," Chance said as he paced back and forth in front of the two teenagers, who were now the ones sitting on Kylie's sofa. To say they were in the hot seat was an understatement. "Are the two of you saying you aren't madly in love and that you never were?"

It had taken the kids twenty minutes to explain to their parents what it had only taken ten to confess to Donovan a few days ago. But Kylie and Chance had stopped them periodically to ask questions.

"Yes, Mr. Steele, that's what we're saying.

Marcus and I are good friends and have been since the first day I started at Myers Park High. One day while talking we decided that neither you nor my mom had a life that didn't center around us, so we decided to give you one," Tiffany said, smiling.

Chance frowned. "You decided? Just like that?"

"Yes, sir, we decided just like that. Wasn't that cool?"

Kylie came to stand next to Chance. "No, that wasn't cool. Did it ever occur to either of you that we liked the life we had?"

"Yes, it did occur to me, but then I wondered what you would do when I left for college in a few years, Mom," Tiffany said quietly. "Just the thought of you being here all alone almost made me give up the idea of leaving home and going off to school. But then I figured it wouldn't be fair for me to give up my life just because you didn't have one. So I decided to help you find one. And when Marcus mentioned how handsome his dad was, and I told him how beautiful you are, we decided the two of you would make the perfect solid soul."

Chance lifted a confused brow. "Solid soul?"

"Yes, it's where two souls combine into one. A very solid one that can withstand anything."

Kylie crossed her arms over her chest and

glared at them. "The two of you deceived us. You had us almost pulling our hair out by pretending you were so much in love."

"We kept asking you to trust us, Ms. Hagan," Marcus spoke up and said. "Even if we were in love, Tiffany and I had been raised right. You and Dad have done a good job. We know right from wrong and we know what to do and what not to do. We kept telling you and Dad that, but you wouldn't listen."

"That's beside the point. What the two of you did last night was—"

"Necessary, Mom," Tiffany cut in and said. "I'm not a child. I knew you were beginning to really like Mr. Steele. I could tell. And I could also tell that you wouldn't let yourself like him fully because you probably thought I wouldn't go along with it when all I ever wanted was someone to come into your life and treat you nice, take you places and make you smile. And Mr. Steele made you smile, Mom. I've never seen you smile so much as when you were around him or talked to him every night on the phone. And I knew our plan was working because Marcus said his dad was smiling, too."

Marcus picked up their defense. "But we also knew something happened, Dad, that weekend Tiffany and I went out of town. When I got back to town the smile was gone and you were acting like you had lost your best friend. Tiffany told me that her mom was acting the same way so we figured the two of you had had an argument. We knew we needed to do something."

Chance sighed deeply. "Is that the reason for the stunt the two of you pulled last night?"

"Yes," Tiffany said softly. "I figured if you cared for my mom that you would come over and make sure she was okay. And you did just what I knew you would do, Mr. Steele."

"In other words, we played right into your hands," Chance said, frowning.

"No, you played right into each other's hearts," Donovan said, coming to stand next to Chance. "I think you've drilled them long enough, and yes, I let them talk me into being a part of their shenanigans because I saw the same thing they did. The two of you cared for each other and you *were* smiling a lot, Chance, when you were together." Donovan grinned. "You were even smiling when you weren't together. You don't know how many times when we were in your office for a meeting that Bas, Morgan and I were tempted to slap that smile off your face. The two of you were meant to be together."

"That's not the point," Kylie snapped.

"Then what is the point?" Donovan asked crossing his arms over his chest. "Your kids cared enough about the two of you to do something. I admit their plan might have needed a little polishing but what the hell. It worked, didn't it?"

The room got quiet. Chance met Kylie's gaze and held it for a long moment. Then he said, "Yes, it worked. Only thing, Marcus and Tiffany, I really don't *like* Kylie. And the reason I don't like her is because I'm deeply in love with her. There's a difference."

Both Tiffany and Marcus smiled and pumped their fists in triumph. "Yes!"

"And how do you feel about my dad, Ms. Hagan?" Marcus asked a few moments later. Kylie knew all eyes were on her, especially Chance's. He knew she loved him. She had admitted as much— but she had also declared that she wouldn't act on that love. Now he was waiting to see if she would reconsider.

What he didn't know was that she had reconsidered the exact moment she had opened the door to him last night. He had come to her when she had needed him most. He had been there with her and had shown her just what a dependable man he was.

And something else. What he'd told her was true.

For the past fifteen years she had been trying to be a good girl for her parents. But even her daughter had been able to see something that she hadn't. She needed a life that didn't revolve around Tiffany or her parents. She was a grown woman and if she made mistakes they were hers to make.

She slowly took the couple of steps that brought her in front of Chance. "And I love your dad, too, Marcus. I discovered just how much I cared for him that weekend and it scared me because I didn't think I was ready to take such a big step as that."

"And are you ready now?" Chance asked her quietly, taking her hand in his.

She held his gaze and said softly, "Yes, I'm ready."

Again Marcus and Tiffany grinned.

"Okay, time for me to take the two of you out for breakfast," Donovan said, sensing his brother and Kylie needed to be alone. "And since we won't be playing our basketball game today, I'll go pick up Bas and Morgan and we can work out our competitive frustrations on the video games."

"That's a wonderful idea," Marcus said, rushing for the door. "And now that Dad knows there's nothing going on with me and Tiffany, I can give Rhonda Denton my phone number."

"And I can give Brad Reagan mine," Tiffany added, following right on Marcus's heels.

Donovan turned to his brother and chuckled. "Boy, the two of you will have a lot to deal with after you get married, with two dating-age teens in the house." He then patted Chance on the back. "We're leaving so the two of you can settle things."

Chance gave his brother an appreciative nod. "And give us a courtesy call before you come back."

Understanding completely, Donovan laughed before he walked out the door, closing and locking it behind him.

"You admitted that you love me in front of them," Chance said huskily, still holding Kylie's hand in his. "I didn't think that you would."

She nodded. "I had to because it's the truth and I couldn't pretend otherwise."

"You know what this means, don't you?"

Yes, she knew what this meant. Chance had told her once that if there was something that he wanted, he wouldn't give up until he got it. "Yes, I know and now, since you have me, what are you going to do with me?"

He smiled that sexy smile that could make her heart race and make her dizzy. "My long term goal is to marry you by next summer, if not before. But my short-term goal is to make love to you, right here and now."

And with that said he captured her mouth in a soul-searing kiss that left her trembling. And then he began removing her clothes as well as his own.

"No visitors and no kids for a while," she whispered when he had gotten her completely naked and stretched out on the sofa.

He smiled. "I would go get the caramel topping but that would be too messy, so I'm just going to have to use my imagination."

He did and enjoyed taking the long, lazy swipes of his tongue over every inch of her body, liking the sound of her moaning and groaning while he did so. By the time he had slid back up her body he knew he was about to take her in a way he had never taken her before. He had already slipped on the condom and the moment he was poised between her thighs, he looked down at her and remembered the term Tiffany had used.

Solid soul.

And as he began sinking deep within her silken heat, he knew that the love the two of them shared was solid soul. It was also something else. It was a love meant to be. A love destined to last a lifetime. A love forged in steel.

He lifted his head and looked into her eyes, then whispered a heartfelt request. "Marry me, baby."

Kylie smiled at him and when he hit her G-spot at an angle that made her moan deep in her throat, he smiled and asked softly, "Was that a yes?"

Her darkened eyes took on a positive gleam when she tightened her arms around his neck and groaned a resounding, "Yes."

Epilogue

Chance couldn't wait until the summer. He and Kylie were married on Christmas Day in the presence of family and friends. Considering how they had met, it seemed very fitting for Marcus to be his best man and Tiffany to be Kylie's maid of honor.

The deafening sounds of cheers, catcalls, whistles and applause shook the room when Chance pulled Kylie into his arms and kissed his bride. It was evident to anyone looking on that the two of them were in love and extremely happy.

At least it was evident to everyone but Cassandra Tisdale. She leaned in and angrily whispered to Bas, "I can't believe he married her when he had a chance with my cousin Jamie. Jamie is a lot prettier and has a lot more class. Kylie works at a florist for heaven sakes! Chance is the CEO of one of the largest corporations in Charlotte. He needs a wife that will complement him."

Bas stared at her, not believing anyone could be that rude or snobbish. But he was seeing a side of Cassandra that he'd always seen. For some reason he'd convinced himself that he could live with it, but now he knew there was no way in hell he could. He wanted to one day have the same thing his brother had—a marriage built on love and mutual respect.

"So you don't think them loving each other is enough?" he asked after taking a sip of his wine.

She gave a ladylike snort. "Of course not. Love is never enough and no one should foolishly think otherwise. According to my mother, who as you know is an expert on social decorum, a good wife, one with the proper breeding like I have, is to be seen and not heard. Her manners and refinements are so ingrained that her husband knows her job is to keep the household running smoothly and make sure they establish the perfect family tree."

Bas lifted a brow. "The perfect family tree?"

"Yes, when they have children. Everything has to be skillfully planned."

Bas thought he'd heard enough. He really didn't give a damn for manners and refinements. Hell, he would settle for a woman oozing in scandal and sin to one who was nothing but a boring social trophy. And he would definitely prefer to come home every night to a wife who would be wearing sexy lace nighties than to one in a starched, buttoned-up-to-her-neck gown.

He shook his head knowing that later, when he took Cassandra home, he would give her the ultimate blow. There was no way in hell he would marry her. "Come on, they're about ready to cut the cake."

"It's not much of a cake if you ask me."

He had heard enough. "I don't recall anyone asking you, Cassandra. If all you're going to do is find fault and be negative, then I'd rather you keep your damn refined and proper mouth closed."

Bas smiled, certain his statement had pretty much shut her up for a while.

Across the room Chance pulled Kylie into his arms. "I love you, Mrs. Steele."

She smiled up at him. "And I love you, Mr. Steele." She then leaned over and whispered, "So what do you think of my parents?"

He smiled. "I can deal with them. They might have preferred you as their good little girl, but frankly I'd rather have you as my bad one. In fact, I plan for the two of us to get downright naughty tonight."

"You plan on teaching me some more moves?" she asked saucily.

"Yeah, among other things."

Kylie's gaze tangled intimately with his. After this small reception they would catch a plane for Hawaii. Chance's parents had returned for the wedding and volunteered to watch Marcus and their newest grandchild Tiffany, who they were anxious to get to know.

"We are going to make one big happy family," Chance said, leading Kylie over to the cake they would be cutting together.

"Yes," she agreed as she paused to place a kiss on her husband's lips. "One big happy family."

* * * * *

*And don't miss Brenda Jackson's next
Kimani Romance title NIGHT HEAT.
Sebastian Steele learns to mix business and
pleasure...in this second episode of the*
Forged of Steele *series.*

FORGED OF STEELE

The sizzling miniseries from
USA TODAY bestselling author

BRENDA JACKSON

*Sebastian Steele's takeover of
Erin Mason's fledgling company
topples when Erin takes over
Sebastian's heart*

NIGHT HEAT

AVAILABLE SEPTEMBER 2006
FROM KIMANI™ ROMANCE

Love's Ultimate Destination

AVAILABLE JANUARY 2007
BEYOND TEMPTATION

Leila Owens didn't know
how to love herself let alone
an abandoned baby
but Garret Grayson knew
how to love them both.

She's My Baby

Adrianne Byrd
(Kimani Romance #10)

AVAILABLE SEPTEMBER 2006
FROM KIMANI™ ROMANCE
Love's Ultimate Destination

Available at your favorite retail outlet.